Lisa Graff

AUTHOR

The Thing about George

TITLE

DUE | BORROWER'S NAME

Mr. Flynn

SCHOLASTIC INC.

New York Toronto London Auckland Sydney
Mexico City New Delhi Hong Kong Buenos Aires

ISBN-13: 978-0-545-11171-3
ISBN-10: 0-545-11171-4

12 11 10 9 8 7 6 5 4 3 2 1   8 9 10 11 12 13/0

Printed in the U.S.A.   40

First Scholastic printing, September 2008

Typography by Jennifer Heuer

To Robert and David

I need you to do me a favor. Yes, you. You'd better do it, too, because I'm not going to let you read any further until you do. Okay, are you ready? Stretch your right arm high up to the sky. Now reach across the top of your head and touch your left ear. Did you do it? Good. Go find a mirror and look at yourself.

Do you see how your arm forms a kind of arch over your head like that? Did you ever realize that your arm was so flexible or that it could reach so far? Did you know you could do that?

Well, Georgie can't.

I thought you should know that before you started

reading about him. It's not that Georgie's problems all started because he couldn't touch his left ear with his right hand, but the fact is that he can't. Even if he wanted to.

You can let go of your ear now.

Georgie sat at his desk in Mr. Myers's fourth-grade class, his chin in his hands, and tried to ignore the tapping on his shoulder.

Tap-tap-tap.

The thing about Jeanette Wallace, Georgie thought, was that she was mean. That's why everyone called her Jeanie the Meanie. Georgie had known her since he was five years old, in kindergarten, and she'd been mean even then. She was always staring at him or following him around at recess and asking him mean questions like "How come your head's so fat?" And when he tried to ignore her, like all the adults in the world told him to, she got mad and bugged him more. Once she'd even made up a song about him.

Georgie Porgie puddin' and pie
Too bad you're only two feet high

True, she'd gotten in trouble for singing it and had to scrape gum off the bottoms of the desks for an entire lunch period, but that still didn't make Georgie feel a whole lot better.

The worst part, though, was that Georgie had been sitting directly in front of her since the first day of fourth grade.

Tap-tap-tap.

Georgie stared straight ahead and tried to think good thoughts, like the fact that this was the last day before Christmas break, which meant no more Jeanie the Meanie for two whole weeks.

Tap-tap-tap.

Suddenly something caught Georgie's eye. Three rows up and two seats over, Andy Moretti dropped his pencil on the floor. Georgie held his breath. If Andy picked the pencil up in one swift movement, it meant the drop had been an accident. But if Andy struck the pencil twice on the floor before returning it to his desk, it was a signal.

The thing about Andy Moretti, Georgie figured, was that he was Italian. Not just a little Italian like Georgie was a little bit Irish (and a little bit German and Scottish and Native American and who knew what else); Andy was *all* Italian. He was also the best soccer player out of all the kids in fourth-grade lunch and Georgie's best friend since forever.

Andy struck the pencil twice.

Georgie smiled and raised his hand. He tried to raise it as high as he could, so Mr. Myers would be sure to call on him.

"Yes, Georgie?" Mr. Myers said. "Did you want to work out this problem for us?"

Georgie nodded and slipped out of his seat to walk to the chalkboard. He hopped up onto the step stool that was always at the front of the room, just for him, and then he finished the problem that Mr. Myers had written on the board: $3 - 10 = -7$.

On the way back to his seat, Georgie made a

detour so he could pass Andy's desk, and Andy slipped a note into his hand. Georgie waited until he was safely back in his seat and then unfolded the paper quickly under his desk. "My mom will pick us up. Don't take the bus!"

Georgie felt another tap on his shoulder. "What's the note say?" Jeanie the Meanie hissed in his ear. Georgie didn't answer. He shoved the paper into his pocket and ignored the tapping until the bell finally rang three minutes later. Then, like everyone else, he leaped out of his chair, snagged his backpack from his cubby, and raced over to the wall by the door to grab his coat.

Everyone in Mr. Myers's class had their own hook for their coats with their name written above it, but Georgie's was different. Georgie's hook was a foot lower than all the others. The janitor had put it in especially for him on the first day of fourth grade. Georgie usually didn't think much about it. He didn't usually think about the step stool under the chalk-board either. Or the fact that his feet didn't reach the floor when he sat at the lunch table, or that Jeanie the Meanie picked on him more than anyone else in the school. That was just the way things were, and Georgie knew there wasn't anything he could do to change it.

Because the thing was, Georgie Bishop was a dwarf.

I need you to do me another favor. I need you to sit down on the floor. Don't worry if it's a little dirty. You won't be there too long.

Now stretch your legs out in front of you, and pull your knees up to your chest. Wrap your arms around your legs, and rest your head on your knees for a second. Then take a couple of deep breaths, in and out. It's pretty relaxing to sit with your head on your knees like that, right? I bet you sit like that a lot, maybe when you want to think for a little bit or when you're waiting for something to happen. You probably think that it's no big deal, that everyone can do it.

Well, Georgie can't.

It doesn't bother him, really, not to be able to rest his head on his knees when he needs to do some thinking. But the thing is, he can't. Even if he wanted to.

You can get up now.

"No more homework! No more homework!" Andy chanted as he and Georgie raced across the icy parking lot to Mrs. Moretti's car. Their backpacks were lighter than they'd been in weeks.

"Hello, boys," Andy's mom greeted them as they piled into the car. "Are you glad it is vacation?" Mrs. Moretti had a thick accent, and Georgie always liked the way she made English sound like a foreign language.

"No more homework!" Andy cried again. Georgie laughed.

When they got to Andy's house, Georgie called his mother to let her know where he was, but he kept his coat on and zipped up. Andy did too. As soon as Georgie hung up the phone, the boys sped right back out the door.

For the past three weeks Georgie and Andy had been running their own business, to raise money for Christmas presents. It had been Georgie's idea. He figured he was getting too old to give his parents just Christmas cards he made in school, and he still wanted to spend his allowance on comics. So he'd decided that he and Andy should start a dog-walking business after school. He knew Andy would agree to it, since he loved dogs but couldn't have one because his dad was allergic.

"Did you decide what you're gonna do with all the money when you get it?" Georgie asked Andy on the way to Mrs. Kipp's house. Today was Friday, payday.

"Yeah," Andy said. "I've been saving up for Galactic Traitors. You know, that new game? Well, that's if I don't get it for Christmas. If so, then I'll probably buy Starbase Invasion 7."

"Cool," Georgie said. He didn't know too much about video games, since he couldn't really play them. He had trouble working the controllers, so all he could do was watch while Andy played, and that wasn't much fun.

They knocked on Mrs. Kipp's door, and she

handed them Buster, her cocker spaniel. "Be sure you bring him back before he gets too cold," Mrs. Kipp told them while Georgie fastened on Buster's leash.

Fifteen minutes later they were walking all six of their dogs. Georgie always walked the small ones, and Andy took charge of the bigger ones. One time Georgie had tried to hold on to Tanya, the Great Dane, but when she'd caught sight of a squirrel, she'd run so fast that Georgie thought she was going to rip off his arm. So now he stuck with Buster and the two poodles, even though he thought poodles were too fancy for their own good. But at least they didn't yank too hard at their leashes.

"So you know what I was thinking?" Andy said as they waited for Apollo, the golden retriever, to sniff a tree.

"What?" Georgie asked.

"Well, I think there's probably a lot more dogs in this neighborhood. Maybe twenty even. We could be making way more money."

"Yeah, but how are we gonna walk twenty more dogs?"

"We could get another partner," Andy said, "to help us out."

Georgie raised an eyebrow. "Like who?"

"What about that kid Russ?" Andy asked. "I told him about it, and he said it sounded cool. He said he wanted to help." Andy had to stop talking for a second to untangle Apollo's and Tanya's leashes. "So?" he continued after a minute. "What do you think?"

Georgie let out a long breath and watched as it left his mouth like a cloud in the cold air. "I don't know," he said. "I mean, I don't really *know* Russ."

Russ Wilkins had moved to their town about a month ago. He was in Mr. Myers's class too, but all Georgie really knew about him was that he had hair that was so blond, it was almost white. That, and the fact that he was an awesome basketball player. Georgie had watched him at recess, when he'd made eleven free throws in a row.

"He's cool," Andy said, his boots crunching in the snow as he walked. "You'd like him. I hung out with him the other day when you were sick."

All of a sudden Georgie knew that he did *not* want

Russ to be their new partner. He'd rather have anyone else, even Jeanie the Meanie, but not Russ Wilkins. He looked down at the dogs, trying to think of something to say.

"I don't think it's a very good idea," Georgie said. "I think it should just be us. Otherwise we'd have to split the money, and we wouldn't be making more anyway."

Andy nodded slowly. "Yeah, I guess," he said. He sounded disappointed, and Georgie didn't like it.

They were silent for a long time after that. They just walked the dogs and watched them sniff trees and didn't say anything. Georgie was about to tell Andy that, Fine, if he *really* wanted to, he guessed Russ could join their business, but only once a week maybe. But right as Georgie was opening his mouth, Andy spoke.

"I think Buster's getting cold," he told Georgie. "We should probably go back."

"Yeah," Georgie said. "I think the poodles are starting to freeze too."

Andy laughed. "They're pup-sicles!" he said.

Georgie snorted so hard he had to wipe his nose. "Poodle-pops!" he said in between laughs.

By the time they'd returned all the dogs and had money bulging in their pockets, Andy seemed to have forgotten all about Russ Wilkins. Georgie was glad he hadn't said anything. Dog walking was definitely better with only two people.

All right, this one's important. I want you to measure some things. First you need to find a tape measure. A ruler would work too.

Okay, are you ready? Good, because I have a list for you. You have to fill in all the blanks.

The distance from the floor to:

the doorknob on my bedroom door=_____
                                   inches
my light switch=_____
                 inches
the edge of my windowsill=_____
                            inches
the faucet on my bathroom sink=_____
                                 inches
the kitchen table=_____
                   inches
the freezer door=_____
                  inches

Don't put the tape measure away yet, because I need to you to measure one more thing. Yourself. Just stand against a wall and have someone mark your height with a pencil. You probably want to do it pretty lightly because I don't want you to get in trouble for writing on the walls. That happened to me one time.

So, how tall are you?

The distance from the floor to:

the top of my head=_____
                    inches

Now make one other mark on the wall, exactly forty-two inches off the ground.

That's how tall Georgie is.

Look at that list again. Would Georgie have to stand on his tiptoes to see out your bedroom window? How easy would it be for him to brush his teeth at your bathroom sink? Would he need to pull over a chair if he wanted to get some ice cream out of your freezer?

I think you should keep all that in mind.

15

When Mrs. Moretti dropped Georgie off at home, his mom was giving a piano lesson, so he gave her a quick hug and then went to his room.

He pushed up on the lever attached to his light switch, dumped his backpack on the floor, and jumped up the set of wooden steps to plop onto his bed. He lay on his back with his hands behind his head, trying to decide on the best way to spend his money.

If he got his parents nice presents, like maybe a really great tie for his dad to wear to concerts and some perfume or something for his mom, they'd probably like it a lot and think he was the greatest son on the whole planet, but he'd have a lot less money to spend on comic books. Maybe he should just get them one thing together. They'd probably like it just as much, and it would be cheaper too. He just had to decide what.

While he thought, Georgie stared at his walls.

Before he was born, Georgie's parents had fixed up his room, doing what many parents do when they prepare for a new baby: They painted the walls a calm shade of blue, put up brand-new curtains, and bought all new furniture. Of course, afterward, when they realized that Georgie wasn't just like other parents' kids, that he wasn't growing the way he was supposed to, they had to change things around a bit. They added levers on the light switches and bought a special low desk and a dresser, just for him. But the poem stayed the same.

Georgie's parents had written the poem themselves. They said they'd worked on it for days before they even started painting, making sure every line was perfect. The poem was written at the very top of the wall, in curving lines, right near the ceiling, and it wove all around the room. Georgie had read it so many times that he had the whole thing memorized.

Where's that fellow with the cello?
Where's the czar who plays guitar?
Where's the harpist who looks sharpest?
We must find out where they are!

Are you nimble with the cymbal?
Do you like to play trombone?
Grab your trumpet! Grab your tuba!
You can bring your xylophone!

Choose the instrument that suits you,
Pack your things, and come along.
Everyone is waiting for you—
Only you complete our song.

His parents had even painted little pictures to go with it, around the waves of the words. There was a miniature tuba and a small brown cello. On lazy Saturday mornings, when Georgie was awake but not quite ready to get out of bed, he would lie with his covers snuggled up to his chin and read the poem over and over, trying to think up rhymes of his own. He'd come up with a few, like "Where's the chum who plays the drum?" but none of them were as good as the lines his parents had written for him. Georgie was certain that one day he'd find a rhyme all his own, one that was good enough to paint right up there with his parents' poem.

Maybe that's what he could do for Christmas—write his parents a poem. That wouldn't cost anything at all.

All at once Georgie noticed that out in the living

room, the clunky notes of the piano lesson had stopped and there was a new sound drifting in, the sound of his parents tuning up. Georgie leaped out of bed to go listen.

The thing about Georgie's parents was that they were musicians, real professional musicians, in a symphony orchestra. They had been since before Georgie was born, so he'd been surrounded by music his whole life. His mom always liked to say that when he was a baby and the doctor asked what she was feeding him, she replied, "Mozart, Vivaldi, and strained carrots." It wasn't like Georgie was some kind of classical music *geek*, though. He knew all about the latest bands, and whose hair was cool now, and what the lead singer of Trepidation's favorite kind of Pop-Tart was. He just happened to like classical music too.

Andy didn't. Not at all. In fact, Andy had been to only one concert with Georgie, and afterward he'd said that he'd rather eat his *nonna*'s chicken neck special for a week straight than be bored out of his mind like that again. He said it would be cooler if Georgie's parents became rock stars.

Well, maybe so. But as Georgie snuggled into the corner of the couch with a blanket wrapped around him and listened to his parents begin to practice, he couldn't help thinking that things were nice just the way they were.

If Georgie were an artist—if he didn't have stubby little fingers, that is, and could hold his pencil like any regular person and make it move where he wanted to—he knew exactly what he'd get his parents for Christmas. He would draw a picture, a really beautiful one, of his mom and dad playing their instruments.

He closed his eyes and pretended for a second that he *was* an artist. In his mind, he made his hand trace out the lines he would draw, exactly the way he wanted them. He started sketching his mom first. He drew her sitting down, tall and elegant, neck stretched proudly, her gigantic harp standing even taller in front of her. He carefully traced her long arm as it reached out to pluck a string he hadn't drawn yet.

Georgie's dad played the cello, which was nowhere near as tall as his mom's harp but was still taller than Georgie. Squeezing his eyes closed a little tighter,

Georgie pretended to sketch out his father, left hand on the neck of his cello, right hand drawing the bow sideways across the string.

As Georgie pretended to draw, his parents kept playing. His mom's notes were quick and distinct. Georgie always felt like he could see the notes she played, one by one, as they left the harp like floating droplets of water. The notes from his dad's cello seemed to come out like one long ribbon of music, sweet and deep, and it was hard sometimes to figure out where one left off and another one started.

When his parents finished practicing, Georgie helped them set the table for dinner.

"So," his mom asked, "how was school today?"

Georgie shrugged as he set a plate on the table. "Good," he said.

"Anything exciting happen?"

"Um . . ." Georgie tried to think as he folded napkins. School seemed like a million years ago now, but he knew his mom wouldn't give up until he gave her some solid details. "Mr. Myers said we're going to start working on the fourth-grade play after winter break. We get to write all the parts ourselves."

His mom nodded. "So, what's it about this year?"

"The presidents." Georgie was glad about that. Last year the fourth-grade play had been about vitamins, which was probably the most boring thing ever.

"That sounds great! Who gets to be in it?"

"Kids get to volunteer," he said.

"So are *you* going to volunteer?"

"I'm not sure yet."

What Georgie really meant was no. A big, fat NO. But he didn't want to tell his mother that.

She smiled at him. "You could be George Washington."

Georgie smiled back. He already *was* George Washington.

Well, sort of.

That was his secret, between him and his parents. Georgie's full name was George Washington Bishop. His parents had named him that because they wanted him to grow up to be big and important, just like the first president of the United States. Well, *important* anyway. They said it was always a good idea to have

22

a great person around to push you to do great things yourself. And that's why they gave him such a special name, so he'd have someone great with him at all times, pushing him from the middle.

Georgie knew practically everything there was to know about the real George Washington. In his room he had tons of books about him, even some big fat ones written for adults. Georgie loved that he had a secret connection to the real George Washington. It made him feel that one day he'd do something great, like become the commander in chief of the colonial army or help draft a constitution. And even though his name was with him all the time, none of the kids at school knew that Georgie had someone important hidden inside him. Not even Andy knew it.

"So?" his mom said. "You should volunteer!"

Georgie shrugged again. He really *did* want to be George Washington. He'd thought of it as soon as Mr. Myers had told them what the play was about. But Georgie didn't look anything like the real George Washington. Not at all. Because the real George Washington hadn't been born with a big head, a stuck-out forehead, arms that barely reached his waist, and legs that bowed at the knees. And Georgie was certain that if the real George Washington *had* looked like that, nobody would've listened to him when he ordered his troops to cross the Delaware.

"I'll think about it," Georgie told her.

His dad came in from the kitchen with a plate of pork chops. "Guess what, Alan," Georgie's mom said to him. "The fourth-grade play this year is on the presidents."

"Really?" He raised his eyebrows at Georgie. "You could be George Washington!"

Georgie mustered up a smile and climbed into his special chair, the one that was a few inches higher than all the others. Sooner or later he was going to have to explain to his parents that he did *not* look like George Washington. Luckily his father changed the subject for him.

"Georgie," he said as he spooned carrots onto his son's plate, "I think your mother and I need to tell you something."

Georgie looked up quickly. What was this? It sounded serious. "Okay," he said.

His father set down the plate of carrots and took hold of Georgie's mother's hand. Georgie looked at them curiously. They kept looking at each other, then back to Georgie. What was going on? Was someone sick? Were they moving? *What?*

"Well," his dad said, "what we wanted to tell you . . ." He cleared his throat and glanced at Georgie's mom again.

Georgie held his breath and hoped for the best.

"Georgie," his dad said, "you're going to be a big brother."

Georgie's chin dropped.

Georgie was sitting at the kitchen table, his feet resting on the top rung of his chair. He nibbled on a peanut butter sandwich and listened to the tinks and pings that drifted in from the living room. He smooshed the peanut butter around in his mouth and thought.

The thing about Allison Housman, Georgie realized, was that she was the prettiest girl in the seventh grade. She wasn't just the prettiest girl in her class or the prettiest girl out of all the seventh graders in the school. Oh, no. Georgie was certain that she was the prettiest girl out of all the seventh graders in the entire world. And next year she'd be the prettiest eighth grader. Too bad for any girl who was born the same year as Allison Housman. As far as Georgie was concerned, any other girl could only hope for second prettiest until Allison kicked the bucket or moved to Mars.

But of all the ways that Allison Housman was pretty—standing at the bus stop, tucking her hair behind her ear, even sneezing—the way she was the prettiest was sitting in Georgie's living room, playing piano. Georgie could see her now where she sat, back straight, toes on the pedals, her bright red hair streaming down the back of her blue turtleneck sweater. Georgie's mother leaned over the piano and turned a page in the music book.

"All right, Allison. That was pretty good. You're making progress." She looked at her watch. "Let's try that last piece one more time, okay?"

Allison sat up even straighter and began to play again, as Georgie's mother counted time.

Tin tin tin PONK ting—"two three four"—*bing!*— "two three four"—*tin ti-tin tong PING!*

Allison was definitely pretty, but that didn't make her any good at playing the piano.

"All right, good work!" Georgie's mom said

graciously when Allison finished. "Remember, no lesson next week, okay? So you'll have lots of time to practice." Georgie thought his mother put a bit too much emphasis on that last word.

"Okay." Allison gathered her things and walked toward the door. She spied Georgie on her way out and raised a hand in his direction. "Hi, Georgie."

His heart stopped. He felt the peanut butter sticking to the roof of his mouth. He racked his brain for something wonderful to say. Something perfect and meaningful, so Allison would know how great he was. Even if he was three years younger. And two feet shorter.

"Hi," he said.

She smiled. The peanut butter on the roof of his mouth seemed to melt.

"Well, 'bye. 'Bye, Mrs. Bishop. Thank you. I promise to practice more this time!"

And the door closed. Georgie's heart started back up again.

"You okay?" his mother asked as she entered the kitchen. Georgie nodded. She smiled and filled the teakettle with water. "Did Andy's mom say it was okay to come over?" Georgie nodded again. "I can take you in about twenty minutes. Is that all right?" Georgie continued to nod. His mom ruffled his hair on the way to the stove.

A few minutes later the kettle started to scream at them, so Georgie's mom plopped a tea bag into her mug and poured in the steaming water. She sat down across from Georgie and stirred her tea with a spoon.

Georgie stared at her. He'd been doing a lot of that since last night at dinner: staring at his mother. He kept trying to find something different about her, something new. It seemed like she should look different somehow, with a whole separate person growing inside her. But she didn't. She looked just the same as always.

"Are you okay, Georgie?" she asked. His mom had asked him that about fifty times since last night. So had his dad. Why would there be anything wrong with *him*? He wasn't the one having a baby.

She set her spoon on the table. Georgie picked it up and began absentmindedly clinking out a melody between two water glasses.

"You know," his mom said, "if you want to ask me

any questions, you can. Anything at all. I won't mind."

She had said that at dinner too. Georgie didn't really have any questions to ask, but it had seemed important to his parents that he ask *something*, so he made some questions up. Like would it be a boy or a girl? They didn't know yet. They said they wanted to be surprised. Did he still have to help wash the dishes? They said yes, of course he did. Then Georgie asked when the baby was coming. They said it was due in May. They also said not to worry, because according to the tests, the baby was nice and healthy.

Well, Georgie wasn't worried. What would he be worried about? But what did they mean, *nice and healthy*? Did that mean the baby was *normal*?

Georgie set the spoon down and took a gigantic bite of his peanut butter sandwich.

If his parents wanted to have another kid, a perfectly normal-looking, *nice and healthy* one, great. He didn't care.

"Georgie, are you sure you're okay?"

He smiled up at his mother, peanut butter smeared across his front teeth. "Yup."

"All right," she said.

Georgie finished off the last bite of his sandwich and wiped his face with his napkin. His mother pressed the back of her hand against her tea mug and took a long look at her son. "Why don't you get your stuff together and I'll drive you to Andy's in a few minutes?"

Georgie hopped off his chair and threw his napkin away.

"Hey, Georgie?" his mom called. He turned. "Give me a kiss, huh?"

He walked to his mother and gave her peck on the cheek. Normally he would have thought that was a babyish thing to do, but his mom seemed to need a kiss right then.

A few minutes later Georgie zipped himself into his warm black winter jacket, shoved his hands into his mittens, and headed out the door with his mom. Andy's house was only six blocks from Georgie's, but his mom always drove him anyway. Usually Georgie would've complained about that. It wasn't like he was four years old or something. And it wasn't like walking was a *strenuous activity*, something he had to be careful about because of his bad back.

But today he didn't mind so much. It was cold out anyway, and the sooner Georgie got to Andy's house, the sooner he'd be able to tell him his horrible news about the *baby*. He knew Andy would understand. Andy understood pretty much everything.

As they left the house, a blast of cold air hit Georgie right in the face. He was about to tell his mom that they were sure to get a blizzard just in time for Christmas when something caught his eye. There was a car driving down their street, in front of Georgie's house. It was going very, very slowly, and the driver was staring at Georgie. His nose was pressed so close to the window that he was fogging up the glass.

Georgie was used to getting stared at. People had been staring at him for ten whole years. He always could tell when people saw him for the first time, because they would stare at him for so long, it was like they were checking to make sure their eyeballs were working. Then, when they saw that Georgie had seen them looking, they'd blink and look away quickly like they'd done something wrong.

Really, Georgie couldn't blame them for staring. If he saw a man who was ten feet tall, or a woman whose skin was dyed green, he'd probably stare too, just to make sure it was real. But sometimes he thought that maybe if those people stared just a little bit longer at him, if they didn't blink all at once and get flustered when they saw Georgie looking back—maybe if they really, *really* gave him a good long gaze to drink in every single detail—they'd never have to stare at him again. Once they adjusted their eyeballs, there was really nothing to look at but Georgie. And he knew he wasn't that interesting.

I think that's a good idea actually. The staring. So before you read anymore, you have to do it. And you'll need a watch too. Or a clock. Go find one.

All right, are you back? Good.

On the next page I stuck in a picture of Georgie that I found. Well, it's a drawing, really, but I think it's a pretty good one. I want you to look at it for thirty seconds. At least thirty seconds, but you can look longer if you want. You have to stare as hard as you can. Try to soak up every single detail, and no blinking. Thirty seconds.

Are you ready? Okay, go!

34

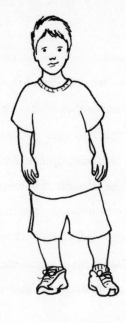

Done looking? Getting bored just staring like that? I guess you can go back to the story then.

The man in the car blinked and sped off down the road, and Georgie climbed into his mom's blue mini-van.

When they got to Andy's house, Mrs. Moretti opened the door before Georgie even rang the bell. She ushered him into the warm house. "Andrea is in his room," she told him.

Georgie tried not to smile. No matter how many times Andy begged his mom *not* to call him Andrea, she simply wouldn't stop.

In a strange way, Andy's real name was the whole reason he and Georgie had become friends in the first place. Not many kids at school remembered it anymore, because when someone is nice and cool and an awesome soccer player, you tend to forget that he has a dumb name. But Georgie couldn't forget. He was there on the first day of kindergarten when Jeanie the Meanie informed the entire playground that Andrea was a *girl's name*.

"No, it's not!" Andy had protested. "It's my grandpa's name!"

"Then your grandpa must be a girl too!" Jeanie shouted.

Andy's grandpa wasn't a girl, of course. He was Italian. In Italy Andrea is a perfectly respectable name for a boy. Georgie didn't know all that at the time. He didn't even know that Andy was Italian. But what he *did* know was that Andy had shared his pretzels at snack time after Georgie had spilled his on the floor. So he felt the need to stick up for him.

"His grandpa's not a girl!" Georgie hollered at Jeanie. "*Your* grandpa's a girl!"

That's when Jeanie the Meanie, already a good six inches taller than Georgie at the age of five, stormed right up to him and stuck her fist in his face.

"You want me to punch you?" she asked him.

Right at that moment Georgie wished he hadn't said anything. No one had really noticed him before, and now here he was, about to get clobbered. Luckily he thought fast. He looked up at Jeanie's angry face and shrugged, pretending he wasn't scared in the slightest. "I guess you could punch me," he said. "But only if your grandpa's a girl."

So Georgie made it through the first day of kindergarten without being punched by Jeanie the Meanie. And ever since, he and Andy had been the very best of friends.

Now Andy sat on the floor in his room with a pile of board games teetering in front of him. He picked up the game on top, glanced at it quickly, and then chucked it into one of the nearby cardboard boxes.

"What are you doing?" Georgie asked from the doorway.

Andy looked up. "Oh, um, I gotta go through my stuff. You know, figure out what I don't need and what I can move to the attic."

"How come?"

Andy sighed. "My *nonna*'s coming."

"So?" Andy's grandmother came to visit from Italy every Christmas. She seemed nice enough, even though Georgie could never understand what she was saying and she kissed his cheeks a lot.

"*So,*" Andy said, rolling his eyes, "she's *moving* here this time. Like forever."

"Really?"

"Yeah. And I have to share a room with her."

"Are you *serious*?" Wow. Sharing a room with your grandma. Georgie couldn't even imagine how horrible that would be. She wouldn't ever let you eat cookies in bed or stay up reading late at night. And what if she snored? "That's awful."

"Tell me about it. So I have to move out all my stuff, to make room for her. Dad's moving another bed in tomorrow. Man! This stinks."

"Yeah." Georgie sat down next to a mound of books. "You want to hear something else that stinks?"

"Is it worse than sharing a room with your grandma?"

"I dunno. Maybe. My parents are having another kid."

"Man!"

"I know."

"That *does* stink."

Georgie sighed. "I know."

"I bet it's gonna have poopy diapers and cry and barf all the time. My cousin did that *nonstop* when he was a baby. He barfed all over everything." Andy chucked another board game into a box and looked up. "Where's it gonna sleep?"

Georgie raised an eyebrow. "I dunno." He'd forgotten to ask that question. "The guest room, I guess. Better not be my room."

"Man!" Andy cried. "That was the best place to play Lava Wars, too!"

"I know."

"This megastinks."

Georgie shrugged. "Yeah." He glanced at the board game on the top of the pile. "Hey, you wanna play Fastest Fishes?"

They played until Andy's mother poked her head into the room and asked them to help decorate the Christmas tree.

At Christmastime the Moretti house was always decorated much differently from Georgie's. The Morettis put up white lights on their Christmas tree, instead of lights of all different colors. They put an angel at the top, instead of a star. They hung sprigs of holly from the corners of every door, and the stockings hanging from the mantel were much longer and skinnier than the ones at Georgie's house. Georgie liked to help out with their decorations. It made him feel like a part of the family. Plus every time he helped, Mrs. Moretti gave him cookies afterward.

Georgie and Andy were squatting on the floor untangling a string of lights, while Andy's father grunted and huffed, trying to put the tree in just the right place. Sweet smells of tomatoes and onions wafted in from the kitchen. As they untangled, Andy and Georgie worked on their new Christmas carol. They wrote at least one new song every year, and so far this year's song went like this:

Jingle bells
Something smells
Prancer ate some beans
And while they flew
He had to spew . . .

But they couldn't think of what came after that.

Mr. Moretti stuck his head out from under the tree, where he was tightening the bolts on the tree stand. "Why would Prancer *spew* if he ate beans?" he asked.

Andy nodded thoughtfully. "My dad's right," he told Georgie. "He'd probably be farting. We're gonna have to rewrite it."

At last the lights and shiny balls were up on the tree, and dinner was ready to eat. Georgie and Andy raced to sit in front of their bowls of ravioli. Mr. Moretti gave his wife a peck on the cheek, there was a unanimous *"Buon appetito!"* from all sides, and then they dove into their meal together. Yep, Georgie thought as he wrapped his tongue around a piece of cheesy pasta, life at the Morettis' was pretty good.

But life at the Bishops' was pretty good too. Sunday afternoon Georgie helped his parents decorate their own Christmas tree. Georgie's dad hoisted him up in the air and let him place the star at the very top. "In our family," Georgie's father always said, "the littlest guy gets to put the star on the tree." Even if it was just a silly family tradition, Georgie liked his job. It made him feel important, like he had a purpose.

Georgie's mother looked up at the star. "Perfect," she said, and Georgie's dad set him back on the floor.

But the moment Georgie's feet hit the ground, he had a terrible, sickening thought. *Next year he wouldn't be the littlest anymore.* Some other kid was going to take his job. Georgie could see it now. New Christmas photos, with some stinky kid in a tiny plaid Christmas outfit holding the silver star in his pudgy little fist. Georgie couldn't take it.

But then he had another thought, one that was even more horrible: *One day he WOULD be the littlest again.*

Why hadn't Georgie ever realized that? One day this kid, the one who wasn't even born yet, was going to be bigger than he was. It wouldn't take very long either; there were five-year-olds the same height as Georgie. Somehow it had never bothered him too much before. Georgie was short, and all those other kids weren't. But the thought of some kid living in his own home, growing taller every single day, made him seriously queasy. Georgie would have to watch it happen. That kid would be able to reach the top of the tree someday without being lifted up. He wouldn't need a special chair to sit in at the breakfast table. He'd be able to ride a bike and reach the top shelf in his closet. And Georgie would just have to sit back and watch the kid outgrow him—inch by inch.

I think you'd better go grab a piece of paper. You can rip a page out of a notebook, if you have one handy, or snag a piece of construction paper. You can even use a paper towel if you want to. You just need something to write on. Oh yeah, and a pen or pencil might help, too.

Got everything? Okay, here's what I need you to do. Figure out what your thing is, and then write it down on that piece of paper. Yeah, your <u>thing</u>. So if you were Georgie, you'd write, "The thing about me is I'm a dwarf." Or if you were Andy, you'd write, "The thing about me is I'm Italian." Or if you were Russ, you'd write, "The thing about me is that I can make eleven free throws in a row."

So whatever it is for you, write it down.

All done? Good. Now fold up your piece of paper and find someplace to hide it, where no one but you will know where it is. In your sock drawer, maybe, or taped to the bottom of your desk. Maybe even inside the shoe you're wearing right now. Just don't lose it, and don't forget where it is. It's important.

Georgie decided that if his parents were going to go do something stupid like have another kid, a kid who would probably end up as huge as Godzilla, he definitely was *not* going to spend his hard-earned dog-walking money to buy them a Christmas present. They were going to have to settle for a nice poem under the tree this year.

Georgie sat himself down at the desk in his room, the one his parents had ordered out of a special catalog, that was just his size and went perfectly with the short chair, so his feet could touch the floor while he wrote. He ripped a piece of paper out of his school notebook and grabbed a pencil from his green soccer mug. Then he began to write.

Merry Christmas, Mom and Dad.
You're my parents and I'm really glad.

He crossed that out and tried again.

Now it is Christmas,
So under the tree
I'm putting a poem
For you from me.

Georgie crumpled the paper and hurled it into the trash can. He ripped out a new page and sat very still, thinking hard. But nothing came. All he could think about was the baby. Baby Godzilla, growing larger and larger inside his mom's belly.

Last night, instead of practicing at her harp like she usually did after dinner, Georgie's mom had settled down on the couch with a book. When Georgie asked her what she was reading, she showed him. It was a book about *babies* and all the stuff parents were supposed to do to get ready for them. It was a really big book.

"Look, Georgie," she'd said, pointing to an illustration in the book, "this is what the baby looks like right now. It says here that the baby is only six and a half inches tall. Isn't that amazing?"

Not really, Georgie thought. But all he'd said was, "Wow. Cool."

Now, on his fresh sheet of paper, Georgie began to write. But without thinking, he wrote something that wasn't a poem at all: "6½ inches."

He pushed his chair back and, still holding his pencil, got up from his desk. Then he walked to his closet and pulled back the door. He kicked away the heap of clothes that had fallen off the hangers—the hangers on the specially installed low bar—and moved the towering stack of old comic books aside. Then he stared at the back of his closet wall.

No one knew it, but long ago Georgie had glued a tape measure to the back wall of his closet. Every year on his birthday Georgie marked how tall he was. And every year Georgie noticed that the marks were getting closer together. Georgie was still growing, but barely.

He stood against the wall, back straight as an

arrow, and marked above his head with the pencil. Then he turned around and looked.

Forty-two inches. Same as before. Exactly the same. He'd hadn't grown a centimeter since August.

Georgie gripped the pencil hard, and kneeling down, he drew another tiny mark, six and a half inches up the wall. Then he stood back and stared at it.

Not even born yet, and Baby Godzilla was already gaining on him.

Georgie shoved his clothes in front of the tape measure and slid his closet door shut with a thud. Then he stormed over to his desk, snatched up the piece of paper—"6½ inches"—and chucked it in the trash can with his rotten poems.

For Christmas, Georgie decided, he was giving his parents cookies.

On Christmas Eve Georgie was lying on his stomach in front of the Christmas tree, inspecting the presents. The cookies he'd baked at Andy's house the day before were safely stowed in the very back of the fridge, behind the milk, with a note on them that said "POISON!" just in case his parents found them early.

He spied a flat box from his aunt Kayla and shook it. No noise. Georgie tossed it aside. It was probably a sweater she'd knitted just for him. Georgie's parents were always saying how hard it was to find nice clothes in Georgie's size, so every holiday that was most of what Georgie got, sweaters. While Andy was showing off his new game system, Georgie was making space in his closet for turtlenecks. His parents usually got him something cool, though. Last year he'd gotten a complete set of Thunder Man action figures. He wondered what he was going to get this year.

Georgie's mom tugged at his shoe and interrupted his gift inspection. "Hey, G," she said, peering at him under the tree, "it's time to get ready for church, okay?"

Georgie headed off to his room.

Normally Georgie wasn't a huge fan of church. He didn't *hate* it or anything, but it wasn't something he really looked forward to. Normally the only thing good about church was the doughnuts afterward. But the Christmas service was different. The church always looked pretty during Christmas, for one thing. There were bright red poinsettias everywhere, and wreaths, and an actual Christmas tree in the lobby with gifts for the poor. Plus they got to sing all of Georgie's favorite Christmas hymns, hymns he actually knew, so he could sing along loud and clear and not have to glue his face to the page just to read the words.

The best part about the Christmas service, though,

was the candles. Every single person who walked into church on Christmas Eve was handed a thin white candle poking through a little ring of paper. At the end of the service, when the minister had finished talking, the person at the end of each pew lit his candle. Then he would help the person next to him light *her* candle by placing the wicks together. Then she would help the person next to her, and so on down the row until all the people in the congregation had a tiny flame flickering just above their fingertips. The lights went out, and the room seemed to glow. And everybody filed outside into the crisp night air, one by one, singing softly as they walked.

And standing outside, tiny white candle in hand, Georgie knew that it was officially Christmas. He would let the candle flicker in the wind for a few seconds, and then he'd blow it out quickly, making the flame disappear in one swift rush. Georgie was pretty sure that was his favorite moment of the night. Perhaps it wasn't *quite* as cool as opening presents the next morning in his pajamas, but somehow, watching the curl of smoke that danced up into the sky, Georgie always felt happy. And he continued to feel that way the whole car ride home, twirling the paper ring speckled with wax dots between his fingers and watching the snowflakes melt slowly on the frosty window.

But even though it was the only time during the year he looked forward to church, Georgie still didn't like the dressing-up part. He headed out of his room a few minutes later with his pants perfectly creased and shirt tucked in nicely all around—and his navy blue tie balled up in his fist. "Dad!" he called. "This stupid tie doesn't work!"

He found his dad in the bathroom combing his hair. "Need some help there?" he asked.

"I think this tie hates me."

Georgie's father laughed. "Ties hated me too when I was your age. Not to worry." Georgie climbed up on the step stool in front of the sink, and his dad whipped the tie into shape. Then he ran the wet comb through Georgie's hair.

"Dad!" Georgie cried. "You're messing it up!" Georgie patted his head, trying to make it look cool again.

Georgie and his father strolled into the living room, and Georgie's mom whistled at them. "Aren't you two looking lovely?" she said. "We all ready?"

Georgie's dad searched his pockets for his keys while his mom went to unplug the lights on the Christmas tree. And just as Georgie's father announced that he had found the keys at last, the house became suddenly dark, and his mother let out a sharp scream.

In an instant Georgie and his dad were halfway across the room.

"What happened?" Georgie's father cried.

"Are you okay, Mom?" Georgie asked.

Georgie's mother rubbed her arm. "I—I'm fine," she said. "I just got a little electrical shock, that's all."

"Did it hurt?" Georgie asked.

She shook her head. "Not too bad." But she looked worried. She squeezed her husband's shoulder. "Alan?" she asked him. "Do you think . . . ?"

"The baby?"

She nodded.

The thing about babies who weren't born yet,

Georgie realized as his parents discussed and worried, was that you couldn't ask them how they were feeling. Or if they'd received an electrical shock. That's why Georgie's mom and dad decided they'd better go to the hospital and check things out, just to be sure.

"Georgie shouldn't have to spend Christmas Eve in a hospital waiting room," his mom said. "Let's call the Morettis and see if he can stay with them for a few hours." And just like that it was decided. Georgie was dropped off at Andy's house, and his parents streaked off in the car to check the health of their precious little Baby Godzilla.

Nonna Rosa greeted Georgie at the door. "Giorgino!" she cried out, arms spread open to welcome him. She stooped down to grab his shoulders and peck him quickly on both cheeks. Georgie gave a forced smile as she babbled at him in Italian, and he resisted the urge to wipe the grandma kisses off his face.

"Georgie!" Andy's mother called as she raced toward him. "Happy Christmas! How is your mother?"

"I think she's okay," Georgie said. "They're just checking Baby G—" He stopped himself in time.

"I mean, the baby."

Mrs. Moretti gave him a reassuring smile. "I'm sure it will be fine," she said.

Andy poked his head out of his bedroom door. "Hey, Georgie!" he cried. "Come help me with something!"

Georgie couldn't believe how different Andy's room looked from the day before. The bed had been moved closer to the door and was covered by a fraying gray quilt. The dresser was piled with antique-looking bottles. And all of Andy's Frantic Fusion posters had been crammed together in one corner above the rollaway bed that now stood against the far wall.

"Wow," Georgie said quietly.

Andy was standing on the rollaway, holding up a blue sheet with fluffy white clouds stamped on it. "I know, huh? We might be moving soon, but until then . . ." He lifted the sheet as high as he could, apparently reaching for the ceiling, but he was still a good foot away.

"Does she snore?" Georgie asked.

"Nah." Andy began to pile all his pillows into one stack in the middle of the bed. "But she does get mad when the room is messy. And she's always trying to get me to speak in Italian." He climbed on the pile of pillows and lifted the sheet to the ceiling again. But just as his hand touched the ceiling, the pillows slipped out from under him and he toppled to the bed. "You wanna help me here?" he asked Georgie.

"Um, what do you want me to do?" Georgie asked as he neared the bed.

"I dunno, maybe like, hold the pillows so they don't keep moving."

"Okay." Georgie held down the mound of pillows while Andy climbed on top again. "What are you doing, anyway?"

"I'm creating a barrier."

"What?"

"I need some privacy, you know?" Andy held the sheet to the ceiling with his left hand and fumbled in his pocket with his right, all the time wobbling on the pile of pillows. Georgie attempted to steady him by grasping his leg. At last Andy pulled out a pushpin and stuck the sheet into the ceiling. Then he jumped down and began moving the pillow pile over a few feet.

When they had finished, the blue sheet was hung crookedly around half of Andy's rollaway bed. But it just wasn't wide enough to hide everything. Georgie and Andy sat on the bed, their backs against the wall, the tips of Andy's toes flicking at the sheet canopy, and stared gloomily at the grandma side of the room that still lay exposed. "Got any other sheets we could use?" Georgie asked.

"Nope," Andy said with a sigh. "They're all on *her* bed."

"Maybe some towels?"

"Don't think they'd be long enough." Andy sighed. "I wish I still had my own room. Russ thought maybe I could move to the attic, but my mom didn't go for it."

Georgie squinted one eye. "Russ?" His voice sounded squeaky. He tried to make it more normal. "When did you see Russ?"

"Oh, I just talked to him on the phone," Andy said. He kept kicking at the sheet, acting like talking to Russ Wilkins on the phone was the most normal thing in the world, like he did it every day. "His parents wanted to know what time our church service was tonight."

"Russ goes to your church?" Georgie asked. Why hadn't Andy ever told him that before?

"Yeah. Anyway, I thought it was a good idea about the attic, but Mom said there's no insulation or something." Andy shrugged. "Oh, yeah, and Russ said he can start helping with the dog walking next week. He even found us two new clients."

"What?" Georgie cried, accidentally banging his head against the wall. He turned to face Andy. "Why did you tell him he could help us? I thought we decided no."

Andy didn't meet Georgie's gaze. He just kept kicking the sheet. "No, *you* decided no." Andy was talking so quietly, Georgie could barely hear him. Georgie didn't think he'd ever heard Andy talk like that before.

"Well, that's because I don't think it's a good idea," Georgie said. "How are we supposed to make more money if we have to split it between three people instead of two?"

Now Andy turned to Georgie. His eyes were wide, and he looked excited. "Because we can advertise!" he said. "That was Russ's idea. If we do that, we can get tons more dogs. Me and Russ can walk all the big ones, and you can walk all the little ones."

Me and Russ. Georgie didn't like the sound of that. He didn't like the idea of Andy and Russ on the phone, talking about all the things they could do together, saying that Georgie couldn't walk any of the big dogs because he was so small, he might get trampled.

"I don't know . . ." Georgie said.

"Oh, come on," Andy replied. "I already told him he could, and I don't wanna be mean. Besides, he's really cool. You'd like him a lot."

Georgie thought about it. He had to admit Russ didn't seem like the type of kid who would make fun of him. Maybe Andy was right. Maybe it *was* a good idea. And it couldn't hurt to make more money.

"All right," Georgie said at last.

There was a knock on Andy's door, and Mrs. Moretti poked her head inside. "Boys, can you—" She stopped. *"Andrea Moretti,"* she said, "is *this* what you wanted my sheet for?"

Andy peered his head out from hiding. Georgie decided he'd rather stay out of view.

"Uh-huh," Andy said. "Mom, I needed some *privacy*!"

She sighed. "Did you put holes in it?"

"Not big ones."

There was a pause, another sigh, and then: "*Va bene.*" Georgie wasn't completely sure what that meant, but from the way Andy's mom said it, he could tell she was giving in. "Come help me set the table," she said. "Georgie too."

For the next hour or so the Morettis kept Georgie pretty busy. He directed traffic in the living room while Andy and his father moved the sofa and Mrs. Moretti and Nonna Rosa set up the folding table. He stood on a chair in front of the stove to stir pots. He folded bright red napkins and set them on the table and climbed up the rickety ladder to the attic to help Andy search for candles. But as busy as he was, Georgie couldn't help thinking about the way Christmas Eve *should* be.

If this were a *normal* Christmas Eve, Georgie realized as he looked at the clock on the wall, he and his parents would just be coming back from church. Then they'd sit down at the kitchen table with regular paper napkins and roast beef sandwiches, because they'd be saving all the really difficult cooking for Christmas Day. After dinner Georgie would be allowed to open just one present before he went to bed. He'd picked out the perfect one, too. A flat, square package he was sure was the *How to Build Homemade Rockets* manual he'd been begging for forever.

He couldn't wait to get home and spend Christmas Eve the *right* way. Every time he heard a car drive past the house, Georgie was sure it was his parents, ready to take him back home before the night was over. But it never was.

It was just past eight o'clock when the phone rang. Georgie held his breath as Mr. Moretti answered it. Could it be . . . ? Georgie couldn't figure out much from Mr. Moretti's side of the conversation. He just kept saying, "Of course, that's not a problem," over and over. Finally he held out the phone to Georgie. "It's your father," he told him.

Georgie grabbed the phone. "Hi, Dad. When are you coming to get me?"

"Hey, kiddo. Look"—he sighed—"we're going to

be here awhile. Everything's fine, but you have no idea how many accidents there are on Christmas Eve. There's this one guy who had a little mishap with a turkey . . . anyway, it might take a long time. I asked Andy's dad, and he said you could spend the night with them if we can't get out of here at a decent hour. Is that okay?"

"Um, I guess so," Georgie said.

"Sorry, Georgie. We'll see you soon, okay?"

"Okay."

"Merry Christmas, G."

"Yeah."

As Georgie ate his way through all the courses of the Moretti Christmas dinner—pasta, venison, potatoes, salad—he couldn't help thinking that right about now he'd be snuggled up on the couch, listening to his parents playing their favorite Christmas songs just for him. His mom would be sitting at her harp, hair swept on top of her head, strumming out a melody with her long, graceful fingers. And his dad would be sitting right beside her at his cello, his bow bouncing out a steady rhythm against the strings, back and forth, back and forth. And Georgie, his toes curled between the cushions of the couch and a blanket pulled up to his chin, would doze slowly off to sleep, not to awaken until Christmas morning.

They had just finished dinner when Mrs. Moretti informed them that they should start getting ready for church.

"Church?" Georgie asked, trying to stay calm. "But it's already nine o'clock."

"Mass is at ten," Mr. Moretti informed him.

Georgie turned to Andy and gave him a look of horror, but Andy just shrugged. "It's not so bad," Andy told him as they put their dishes in the sink. "It's only an hour. Then we get to sleep in late."

Sleep in? That wasn't how it worked. Georgie was supposed to be at *his* house, already asleep on the couch so he could wake up super early, race into his parents' bedroom, and open presents with them while the sun came up and they sipped their coffee. There was no *sleeping in* on Christmas morning. And who in their right mind would go to church at ten o'clock at night? Georgie couldn't believe this.

The entire way to the church Georgie sat squished between Nonna Rosa and Andy, with his arms folded angrily across his chest. He frowned as they walked through the door and all the people who didn't know him smiled like he was *just the cutest little thing ever*. One old man even patted him on the head and asked how old he was. And then—*then*—Georgie caught sight of Russ. Russ and his white-blond hair you couldn't help noticing from a mile away. He waved at them and ran over.

"Hi, Andy!" he cried. "Hi, Georgie! I didn't know you went to this church."

"I'm just visiting," Georgie mumbled.

Georgie shuffled his feet as Andy's parents chatted with Russ's parents, who were both about a billion feet tall.

They all filed into pews and sat down, Georgie next to Andy next to Russ, and all the parents behind them.

Russ leaned over Andy to talk to Georgie. "I have some really great ideas about how to advertise for our dog-walking business," he said.

Our business? Georgie thought. Hadn't it all been

his idea? But he didn't say anything.

As the choir began to sing, Georgie noticed something: There were *no candles*. What kind of church would forget to hand out candles? The one time out of the whole year that church was actually cool, and there were no candles. And *Russ* was here. The only thing worse would be if Jeanie the Meanie were sitting behind him, tap-tap-tapping on his back during the whole service. Georgie hated this church, he decided, this church without candles. He was so angry, he refused to sing any of the songs, even the ones he liked. Of course it didn't help that Nonna Rosa was standing right behind him, singing all the hymns in Italian at the top of her lungs. And he kept getting confused, during the whole service. Everyone else seemed to know when to kneel, and when to stand, and when to start singing, and Georgie kept stumbling along behind. There were Russ and Andy doing everything together perfectly, and there was Georgie looking like a moron. He was sure everyone was staring at him, thinking he obviously didn't belong.

About halfway through the service, Georgie

stopped trying. He sat on the hard wooden pew, his arms folded across his chest. He didn't sing; he didn't follow along with the Bible passages; he just stared at his feet. His tiny little feet in his Velcro-strap shoes. Andy and Russ both had lace-ups.

Favor time. You have to be wearing shoes for this one, shoes with laces, so go put some on if you need to.

All right, you ready? Untie both your shoes. You can put the book down while you do it. I'll wait for you.

Done? Good. Now, I want you to hold your hands out in front of you and curl your fingers, so you can't see past your knuckles. Then, with your fingers still curled up tight like that, I want you to tie your shoes.

I'm serious. Tie your shoes.

Give up yet? I did. I tried to do it for about fifteen minutes. It's really hard. Anyway, that's why Georgie's shoes are Velcro. Just thought you should know.

You can straighten out your fingers now.

When they got back to the Morettis' there was a message on the machine from Georgie's father that said they were still at the hospital. So Georgie would have to spend the night. Which meant he wouldn't be getting his rocket book until late tomorrow morning. And he wouldn't be able to leap onto his parents' bed to wake them before the sun came up. It was his last Christmas ever without Baby Godzilla around, and it was ruined. Completely ruined. Things would never be the right way again.

Andy lent Georgie a pair of pajama pants—the smallest pair he owned—but they were way too big, and Mr. Moretti had to give him the tie from his bathrobe to keep them up. Georgie stood at the sink in Andy's bathroom, on the step stool that the Morettis had bought years ago, just for him, and brushed his teeth next to Andy. Andy had a toothbrush. Georgie had to use his finger.

"Should we sleep in my room or in the living room?" Andy asked between spits.

"Living room," Georgie said. Usually they slept in Andy's room. They'd trade off turns for the bed, and whoever had to sleep on the floor got the comfiest pillow. But Andy's room felt like a grandma room now, and Georgie didn't think he'd ever get used to that.

"Okay," Andy said, rinsing off his toothbrush. "I'll get the sleeping bags."

As Georgie and Andy nestled into their sleeping bags in the living room, with the pine scent of the Christmas tree looming over them, Georgie couldn't help noticing that the feet lump in his sleeping bag was much higher up than Andy's. He wondered if Andy ever noticed stuff like that.

"So what'd you think about those flyers?" Andy asked.

Georgie mashed his pillow into a comfortable ball and turned to look at Andy. "Huh?" he said.

"Those flyers Russ was talking about. You know? Advertising. For our business. Don't you think Russ should do that? Draw dogs on it and everything? He's a good drawer."

"It's *my* business," Georgie said.

He hadn't planned on saying it; it just came out. But as soon as he said it, he was glad he had. Because it was true.

"What?" Andy asked.

"It's my business," Georgie said again. "I thought of it, so I should be in charge of advertising. And I don't think we should have advertising."

"But Russ says—"

"And Russ can't be in it either. I decided."

Andy sat up in his sleeping bag. It was dark, so Georgie couldn't see his face. He was kind of glad about that.

"That's not fair," Andy told him.

"Too bad," Georgie said. He rolled over and faced away from Andy, toward the tree. "It's my business."

Andy was silent for a long time, and Georgie didn't know what to think. He was starting to wish he hadn't said anything.

"Maybe I'll start my own business then," Andy said at last.

"Fine," Georgie said.

"Fine," Andy replied. "And *Russ* will be in it with me. And we'll walk four *thousand* dogs. And we'll leave all the poodles for you."

Georgie could feel his face burning. Andy had never said anything like that to him before. Never.

Georgie curled the edge of the sleeping bag up to his chin and stared at the Christmas tree as he spoke. "Maybe your *grandma* can help you too," he said. "Your smelly old grandma, who stinks up your whole room."

Behind him Georgie could hear Andy thrashing around in his sleeping bag for a few seconds before it was completely quiet again. It was quiet for a long, long time. Georgie waited for Andy to say something, but he didn't. And when Georgie turned around to see if he'd fallen asleep, Andy wasn't there. His sleeping bag was empty. He must have gone to sleep in his room—his *grandma's* room—and left Georgie all alone on the living room floor on Christmas Eve.

Georgie hardly slept at all that night. He kept thinking about how he should go apologize to Andy. He
almost did it a hundred times. Once he even walked all
the way to Andy's room, and he was totally ready to
walk right in and tell Andy he was sorry, but then he
remembered Nonna Rosa. Wouldn't she be mad if
Georgie woke her up in the middle of the night? So
Georgie went back to his sleeping bag.

As the night wore on, Georgie figured out whose
fault everything was. It sure wasn't his: The dog-
walking business *was* his idea; he was right about
that. And it wasn't Andy's fault either, not really.

No, Georgie realized. The whole dumb fight was Baby Godzilla's fault.

If it hadn't been for that stupid not-yet-a-baby baby, Georgie wouldn't have had to spend Christmas Eve at Andy's in the first place. He would have spent it with his parents, the normal way, with everything just how it was supposed to be. And if that had happened, Georgie wouldn't have been so angry when Andy asked him about Russ. He never would've reacted the way he had if Baby Godzilla hadn't messed up his Christmas.

Suddenly, lying there on Andy's floor, his sleeping bag tangled in a heap around his feet, Georgie had a terrible thought. For just one second he hoped that the baby *wasn't* okay, that while his parents were at the hospital, the doctor told them, "I'm so, so sorry," in a very sad voice, and that the baby would never be anything more than a pencil mark six and a half inches up Georgie's wall.

Georgie squeezed his eyes shut tight and tried not to think such horrible thoughts.

As soon as the kitchen clock blinked 6:00 A.M., Georgie padded across to the phone. He called his parents and, in his quietest voice, asked them to pick him up. Then he changed into his clothes from the day before and put on his coat and hat. He wanted to leave a note to Andy to say he was sorry—even if he wasn't completely sure he *was* sorry—but by the time he heard his dad pull up outside, all he'd written was "Dear Andy." He crumpled the piece of paper up and shoved it in his pocket as he raced out the door.

His dad looked tired, and he needed to shave. He forgot to wish Georgie Merry Christmas, but Georgie didn't remind him.

"I think your mom and I need to sleep for a while," he told Georgie when they were pulling into their driveway. "We're going to have to put off presents for a few hours, okay, G?"

"Yeah, okay." Georgie didn't even bother to slam the car door shut. He was too tired.

"Hey, Georgie?" his dad called.

Georgie turned.

"The baby's fine, by the way. I thought you might be worried."

Georgie decided he wasn't too tired to slam the front door, but he made it sound like an accident.

When they finally got around to opening presents around eleven, Georgie went straight for the book on rockets. He needed something to cheer him up. Plus he really felt like making something explode. But when he unwrapped the present, it turned out not to be a book about rockets at all. It was a book called *So You're Going to Be a Big Brother?* And even though later it turned out that Georgie's parents had gotten him a bike—his first bike ever, specially designed for him, with an extra-low seat and easy-to-reach pedals—Georgie wasn't as excited about it as he wanted to be.

"Do you want me to show you how to ride it?" Georgie's dad asked.

Georgie just frowned. "No, thanks," he said. He couldn't make anything explode with a bicycle. "It's kind of cold and snowy out."

"Oh," his dad replied. "Okay then." He sounded disappointed, but Georgie pretended not to notice. "Well, let me know when you feel like taking it out for a spin."

"Sure," Georgie said. And he shuffled off to his room.

All that day Georgie didn't call Andy to apologize, because it was Christmas Day, and you weren't supposed to call people on Christmas Day. Andy was probably doing loads of important stuff with his family anyway, and he wouldn't want to be bothered just for a stupid little apology.

The day after Christmas Georgie wanted to call Andy as soon as he woke up. But he couldn't think of the right thing to say. Should he come right out and tell Andy he was sorry? Or should he just pretend like nothing had happened?

Finally, just after four, Georgie called.

Andy picked up the phone. "Hello?"

"Hey," Georgie said.

"Oh. Hey." Andy didn't seem too excited to hear from him.

"Um . . ." Georgie shifted the phone under his ear, trying to remember what he wanted to say. "You want to come over for dinner? My mom's making tuna casserole." Georgie's mom *wasn't* making tuna casserole, but he figured he could convince her. It was Andy's favorite.

"Oh. Well . . . I can't. I'm . . ."

"What?" Georgie asked.

Andy sighed. "I'm going over to Russ's to watch a movie. He said you could come too if you wanted, but don't worry, I already said no, 'cause I know you don't like him."

Georgie wanted to slam the phone down, but he didn't. Maybe he should have. At least it would have stopped him from saying something dumb. "You're right I don't like him!" he said. He hollered it, actually, quite a bit louder than he'd meant to. "That's 'cause he thinks he's so much better than everyone else." He took a quick breath and said the thing he'd been wanting but not wanting to say for days now: "And you can't be friends with him if you're friends with me."

There was a pause, but when Andy started talking again, he sounded angrier than Georgie had ever heard him. "Well, fine," he said. "Then I won't be your friend anymore. And by the way, we're *moving* this summer, and I hope it's really far away so I never have to see you again!"

"Good!" Georgie shouted. "I hope you do! I hope you move next door to *Russ*, your best friend in the whole world!"

"I will!"

"Fine!" Then Georgie did slam down the phone. But it was much too late.

Moving?

Georgie had to find his parents. They'd know how to fix everything. He found them in the living room, his mom sitting on the couch and his dad in the recliner. He was about to rush into the room and tell them everything, maybe sit next to his mom on the couch and have his parents tell him it would all be

78

okay, but then he stopped. And blinked. And really *noticed* what they were doing.

Georgie's dad wasn't just sitting in the recliner. He was reading. He was reading that stupid fat book about babies. And his mom wasn't just sitting either. She was flipping through a book of knitting patterns. *Knitting?* Since when did his mom *knit?* She had one hand on her belly, too, rubbing it in slow circles.

His dad looked up. "Hey, G," he said, "need something?"

Georgie shook his head and slumped off to his room.

The next afternoon the doorbell rang.

"Georgie, can you get that?" his mom called.

Georgie went to the door. And for a second he had high hopes. What if it was Andy, come to apologize? Maybe things would be all right after all. Maybe . . .

But when Georgie opened the door, he felt his stomach sink. There was no one there. He looked up the street and down, but there was no one at all. And then he saw it. Taped to Georgie's door was a bright yellow flyer.

Right in the middle there were drawings of dogs—really good drawings—and at the bottom was Andy's phone number.

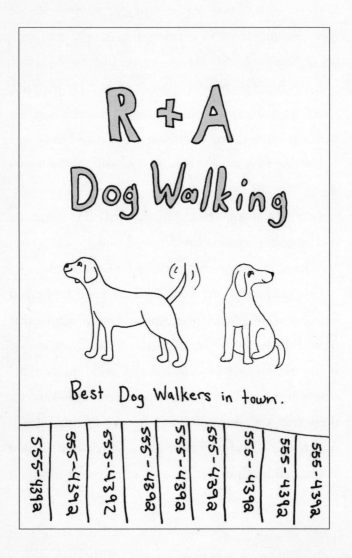

The first day back at school Georgie was sitting at his desk in Mr. Myers's class, with the edge of a pillow poking him in the back while he yanked at a loose thread on his sweater from Aunt Kayla.

When he was at school, Georgie had to sit at a regular desk, not like the special short one he had at home. His chair was regular too, which meant that Georgie didn't quite fit in it. So he had to sit with a pillow behind him, to support his back, and a crate under his feet. Georgie had told his parents a hundred times that he felt stupid sitting like that, and could they *please* tell Mr. Myers that he didn't need all that stuff anymore, but his parents said they were more concerned about his spine than his pride. Whatever that meant.

"Okay, everybody," Mr. Myers announced. "We're going to start working on our presidents project, so I need you all to find a partner."

Normally Georgie would have been excited to find out they were doing a partner project. Normally his head would have shot up as soon as he heard, so he could fix his eyes on Andy across the room. The two of them would have smiled at each other and nodded, the first people in the class to have partnered up.

But today Georgie didn't dare look up. He knew that if he did, if he looked in Andy's direction, that Andy wouldn't be looking back. So he didn't look at all. He just kept tugging at that loose thread.

Georgie hadn't spoken to Andy since that terrible afternoon on the phone over a week ago. He'd spent his whole vacation just hanging around the house, listening to his parents discuss cribs and car seats, 100 percent bored out of his mind. But being at home was way better than being anywhere else, because everywhere he went, it seemed like he saw another yellow flyer for Russ and Andy's dog-walking business. When he went to the grocery store with his mom, there was one tacked to a bulletin board outside. When he was in the car with his dad, he saw three plastered to telephone poles as they drove by. Georgie figured if he wanted to, he really *could* have his own business, like he'd told Andy. He could advertise too: "GEORGIE DOG WALKING: Better than anyone!" But what would be the point? Who wanted to walk a bunch of miniature poodles around in the snow with no one to talk to?

The truth was, Georgie missed Andy. And not just because of the dog walking and making money. He missed Andy's house and Andy's mom's cookies. He missed playing board games and Lava Wars and listening to Andy talk about the latest video game he was trying to beat, when he'd get so excited and talk so fast that Georgie's ears could hardly keep up with the stream of words. Georgie sort of even missed getting kissed on the cheeks by Andy's grandma.

Most of all, though, Georgie missed having someone to talk to. He *needed* to tell someone about Baby

Godzilla, that stupid baby who was ruining his life. He certainly couldn't tell his parents about it.

Georgie's mom and dad had been so busy thinking about Baby Godzilla lately that Georgie was pretty sure they didn't even know he'd had a fight with Andy. Once his dad had asked him why he wasn't walking dogs anymore, but Georgie had just said he didn't feel like it, and his dad left him alone after that. And when his mom suggested that he invite Andy over for dinner, and Georgie told her Andy had the flu, she was so busy knitting a pair of baby bootees that she actually believed him.

Well, maybe his parents were oblivious, but Georgie *knew* he was in trouble. Andy was going to be partners with Russ for sure, and Georgie was going to be left with no one.

Unless . . .

He tugged at the thread. No. He knew Andy wouldn't want to be partners with him. Why would he? Georgie knew he shouldn't even bother to look.

But . . .

There was a little voice in Georgie's head that

thought there might still be a chance, that maybe—just *maybe*—Andy would still pick him. But the whole rest of Georgie's head knew that the little part was crazy.

Still, Georgie thought, *it couldn't hurt to just look.*

So Georgie looked. He lifted his head and found Andy at the front of the room. And as soon as Georgie saw him, he realized it was too late. Andy was looking at Russ. Georgie had been permanently replaced.

He let out a deep breath and shrank back into his seat. Georgie studied the back of Russ's head, one row up and four seats to the left. It made sense, really, that Andy would want to be best friends with Russ. The two of them had more in common than Andy and Georgie had ever had. Andy was a killer soccer player, and Russ was probably the best basketball player in the whole school. Georgie had never even played basketball. Jumping and running weren't good for his back. When they played basketball in PE, Georgie had to walk laps with the asthma kids. It didn't matter anyway, Georgie realized. His hands weren't big enough to hold the ball. He snorted. Who was he kidding? He could *be* the ball.

"Is there anyone who doesn't have a partner?" Mr. Myers asked the class. Georgie slowly raised his hand.

"Okay, then," Mr. Myers said. "Why don't you two partner up?"

You two? Who else was left? Georgie turned around to see.

He couldn't believe it. Behind him, with her hand in the air, was none other than Jeanie the Meanie.

Four days later Georgie and Jeanie were sitting in two chairs squeezed together in front of a computer in the school library. Their whole class was there for an hour, and they were supposed to be looking for books for their projects. Georgie was pretty sure, though, that Jeanie had no idea how to use an online catalog.

"Type in *Lincoln comma Abraham*," Georgie told her for the fortieth time.

Jeanie blew her thick brown bangs out of her eyes and typed in *shoelaces*. Then she pounded the keyboard when the computer screen informed her: "The search produced no results." She typed in *rodents*.

Georgie felt like screaming. "Will you *please* let

me do it?" he said.

"No, wait," Jeanie told him. "I found a lot of stuff this time."

Georgie rolled his eyes. He'd been pretty upset when they'd been assigned Abraham Lincoln and not George Washington, but not nearly as upset as he was that he had to work with Jeanie the Meanie every Friday for six whole weeks.

"Hey," Jeanie told him, in a voice that was much too loud for the library, "did you know there's a book called *Mice Are Nice*? We should check it out."

"Jeanie, will you just let me type?"

"Why, are you gonna look up books about shrimp-azoids like you?"

Georgie narrowed his eyes at her.

"Something in your eye?" she asked.

Before Georgie could tell Jeanie exactly how much he hated her, he noticed Mrs. Chinsky, the librarian, coming over to check on them. He snagged the keyboard out from under Jeanie's hands and started to type in *Lincoln, Abraham*, so they wouldn't get in trouble for goofing off.

"And how's it going over here?" Mrs. Chinsky asked them. "Are you finding everything you need?"

"Oh, yes," Jeanie said. "Did you know your library has twenty-three books about Abe Lincoln?" She pointed to the screen.

Mrs. Chinsky smiled. "Well, I didn't know the exact number," she said.

"It's twenty-three," Jeanie told her.

Georgie hated when Jeanie the Meanie acted nice in front of grown-ups. It made him want to barf. He clicked on a book entitled *Abraham Lincoln: Born to Lead*, and scribbled down where to find it.

"Also, Mrs. Chinsky?" Jeanie went on. "The library doesn't have any books about shoelaces. I checked."

"Is that so?" Mrs. Chinsky replied.

Georgie also hated when grown-ups acted like Jeanie the Meanie was funny, instead of just mean.

"Yeah," Jeanie said. "I think you should get some."

"Well, I'll look into that, Jeanette. Good luck with your project. Let me know if you two need anything."

When Georgie had made a list of the books he thought might be helpful, he and Jeanie went over to the shelves to get them. As they passed through the reference section, Georgie scanned the shelves. He couldn't help it; every time he was in the library, his eyes naturally drifted to a particular book.

It was called *Little in a Big World*, and it was a book about dwarfs. It had been in the library for years, and Georgie was pretty sure that Mrs. Chinsky had gotten it because of him, like if kids wanted to check it out to learn about him or something. Georgie had flipped through it once. It had pictures of dwarfs in it, some who looked a lot like him, and some who didn't at all. It talked about what it was like to be a dwarf, and stuff that was hard and stuff that wasn't. Georgie had looked in the front of the book too, to see who had checked it out, but there were no names on the catalog card. At the time he wasn't sure if that made him happy or not. It kind of stank to know that no one wanted to learn about him, but in a weird way it made him feel a little more normal too, like maybe he wasn't different enough that people thought they *should* learn about him. It was sort of strange anyway, having a book about him in the library. No one else in the entire school had a book about them.

Georgie didn't see the book on the shelf, but he didn't have much time to look either, because Jeanie was starting to drift over toward the section on rodents, and he knew if he didn't catch her quickly, they'd never get anything done.

Georgie and Jeanie were allowed to check out only two books each, so they had to go through and decide which ones were the best. Actually, *Georgie* had to go through all of them, because Jeanie just sat next to him at the round wooden table and doodled on the cover of her notebook with a pencil, humming loudly in his ear.

She stopped humming just as the tip of her pencil broke on her notebook. She grabbed Georgie's pen from his hand. "Mind if I borrow this? Thanks."

Georgie dug another pen out of his backpack and flipped through *Lincoln: Head and Shoulders Above the Rest*, trying to block out the sound of Jeanie's humming. But it was really hard.

"Hey," she said, nudging him with her elbow, "wanna see what I'm drawing?" She held up her notebook, but Georgie didn't look. He turned a page in his Lincoln book and tried to learn about the sixteenth president.

Jeanie nudged him again. "I asked if you wanted to see my pictures," she said. Georgie didn't answer. "You deaf or something?"

"Leave me alone."

"I will when you look at my drawings."

"I'm trying to read."

Jeanie plopped her notebook down on top of Georgie's Lincoln book, so he couldn't read. Georgie pushed the notebook aside.

"Hey!" Jeanie said. "Just look at it. It's good. You'll like it."

"Why don't you read a book like we're supposed to?"

"'Cause I'm *trying* to show you my *art*!" Jeanie held the notebook in front of Georgie's face. "Just look already!"

Georgie looked. On the cover of her notebook, Jeanie the Meanie had drawn a picture of their class. The students were standing in a long row, every one of them, and each picture was labeled with the person's name underneath it. And there, at the end, was Georgie—short arms, fat head, and all.

Georgie swatted the notebook away. "Leave me alone, Jeanie."

Jeanie flared her nostrils for a second and looked like she was going to say something mean, but instead she took up humming again. She put her foot up on the table and began writing on the rubber around the bottom of her shoe. For a second Georgie found himself staring at her rats' nest of hair. Her sloppy ponytail was just off-center, and Georgie wished she'd fix it. It was really starting to bug him. Jeanie the Meanie was the only person in the world who could manage to have annoying hair.

Georgie turned back to his book and tried to concentrate, but Jeanie's humming seemed to be getting louder by the second. Why couldn't he have a partner who actually *did* stuff? He was going to get stuck with all the work, he could tell right now, and when it was all over, and they'd turned in their report, Jeanie the Meanie was going to smile at Mr. Myers and pretend like she'd actually helped. And only

Georgie would know that all she'd *really* done was write on her shoe.

He saw a flash of white hair in the corner of his eye and turned to see Russ and Andy selecting a book off the shelves. They weren't writing on *their* shoes.

Georgie looked back at Jeanie. He should tell her now, before things got out of hand. "Jeanie," he'd tell her, "you gotta do stuff. I'm not gonna do all the work."

But what he ended up saying was "Why'd you write *JAW* on your shoe?"

Jeanie was now doodling a flower on the knee of her jeans. "'Cause that's my initials," she said.

Georgie snorted, and Jeanie's head shot up. "What?" she said.

"Well, that's kind of dumb."

"Is not," Jeanie huffed. She pulled her shoe up to her face to look at it more closely. "Is not," she said again, putting her foot back on the floor. She looked up at him. "Why, what're your initials then?"

Georgie shook his head. "Not telling."

"C'mon." She threatened him with his own pen. "I'll poke you."

"No! Stop it!"

"Then you better tell me."

"No way."

Jeanie raised the pen, poised and ready to jab Georgie in the arm. *"Tell me."*

Georgie rolled his eyes at her. "No," he said.

She glared at him for a second and then set the pen on the table. "Just tell me your middle name," she said.

"No. Leave me alone."

"Mine's Ann."

"I don't care."

"Yours must be *awful*." Georgie could tell she was trying to draw it out of him. It wouldn't work. "Is it Hector?"

"No."

"Gerald?"

"No."

"Bartholomew?"

"No. Just help me look through these books, okay? I'm not gonna do all the work, you know. You have to help too."

"Fine." Jeanie grabbed a book from the middle of the

stack, so that five books toppled to the floor with a loud thud. Georgie could feel his face burn as everyone in the library turned to look at them. He quickly snatched the books up and piled them back on the table. Jeanie sat calmly, puffing out her cheeks as she read.

For about twenty minutes Georgie thought things were going pretty well. He and Jeanie sat quietly, turning pages slowly and picking up new books every once in a while. Just as Georgie put the last book down, Jeanie tugged on his sleeve, and her face looked excited.

"You find something interesting about Lincoln?" Georgie asked hopefully.

Jeanie shook her head. "Nope," she said. "But I think I figured it out."

"What?"

She drew a long black line on Georgie's arm with his own pen and grinned at him. "Your middle name's Alfonso, isn't it?"

Georgie pulled his arm away from her. "No!" he hollered. "Will you shut up? I'm not ever going to tell you." He saw Mr. Myers looking at them from across the room, so he lowered his voice. "Anyway, we're almost out of time. Didn't you find anything yet?"

Jeanie stared at him blankly. "About what?" she asked.

"About Abraham Lincoln," Georgie said. What was *wrong* with her? "The guy we're *studying*."

Jeanie nodded, and her off-center ponytail bobbed up and down. "Oh, yeah," she said. "I found out loads of stuff."

"Like what?"

"Like he was tall and ugly and wore a stupid hat."

Georgie glared at her. "Great. Thanks. That's really helpful."

Jeanie didn't say anything, just went back to drawing the flower on her jeans.

"Well," Georgie said, picking two books off the table, "I'm checking out these two books. You can pick whichever ones you want."

When Georgie got to the librarian's desk, Mrs. Chinsky wasn't there, so he stood and waited. He noticed a metal cart that was stacked high with books ready to be returned to the shelves, and he scanned the titles.

Little in a Big World.

Someone had checked it out! Georgie glanced to the left, then to the right, and as quick as he could, he snagged the book off the cart, turned to the inside cover, and pulled out the catalog card to look at the name.

"Jeanette Ann Wallace."

Georgie snapped the book shut just as Mrs. Chinsky returned to her desk.

"Hi, Georgie," she said. "Did you find some books you wanted to check out?"

He nodded and handed her the two books on Abraham Lincoln.

While Mrs. Chinsky stamped, Georgie thought. Why on earth would Jeanie the Meanie want to check out a book about him? She hated him.

Mrs. Chinsky handed him his books, and Georgie went back to the table. He sat down next to Jeanie and looked at her closely. Should he say something? Should he tell her he knew?

Jeanie was drawing a snake on her jeans now. Its head was reared back, jaws spread wide, ready to swallow the flower. Georgie was just opening his mouth to say something when the bell rang. Jeanie closed her book with a thud.

"Hey, shrimpazoid," she said. "You should close your mouth before you drool on yourself." And she stuck Georgie's pen in her pocket.

Georgie just sighed and leaned back in his chair. That snake, he decided, had some seriously huge fangs.

Time for another favor. I'd like you to pick up a pencil and hold it for a second, the way you do when you're writing. Now look at your hand. See how the pencil falls between your fingers like that, some on top and some on bottom? Probably someone told you to hold it that way, back when you were first learning how to write, and you've never even thought about it since then. I bet you just pick up a pencil and <u>BOOM</u>! Fingers all in place. I bet you think it's really no big deal to be able to hold it like that. I bet you think everyone can do it.

Well, Georgie can't.

When Georgie wants to write something, he holds

his pencil with four fingers wrapped all the way around, the way you'd make a fist. You should try it for a second. Feels kind of funny, doesn't it? But that's the only way Georgie can write, because his fingers are only about half as long as yours. So even things like writing a sentence take a little bit more work than you might think. Same with turning a doorknob or putting a key in a lock, things you might not think twice about. Imagine trying to hold a violin bow with fingers like that.

You can put down your pencil now.

Early Saturday evening Georgie and his parents piled into the minivan, with the harp and cello stowed safely in the back. Georgie's mom was wearing a fancy black dress, with her hair piled up on top of her head, and both Georgie and his dad were wearing tuxedos. Technically, only Georgie's dad had to wear a tuxedo, since Georgie was just going to be sitting in the audience, but ever since Georgie's parents had paid for his custom-made tux for his aunt Kayla's wedding, they tried to get as much use out of it as possible. Georgie didn't mind too much. It sort of made him feel like a member of the orchestra.

Georgie's mom had just put in a CD of Pachelbel's Canon, and they were only a few blocks away from their house, when Georgie's dad pointed out the window.

"Isn't that Andy?" he said.

Georgie looked. It was, in fact, Andy—Andy and Russ, walking five dogs apiece down the sidewalk.

"No," Georgie said quickly. "That's not him."

"I think it is," his mom said. "Why don't we stop for a second and you can say hi?"

"It's not him, Mom!" Georgie shouted.

"Georgie," his dad said sternly, "that's no way to talk to your mother."

"Sorry," he mumbled. He saw his parents give each other a look, but Georgie's dad drove past Andy and Russ without stopping.

When they got to the concert hall and parked in the back, one of the other cello players came out and helped Georgie's dad pull the instruments out of the minivan. Georgie's mom unbuckled her seat belt and turned around to face Georgie. But she didn't say anything; she just looked at him, like she was studying his face in case there was a quiz on it later.

"Mom?" he asked.

She reached a hand out to pat his knee. "Just wondering if everything's okay with you."

"Everything's okay," he said, and looked out the window. It was gloomy outside. He wondered if it would snow again.

His mom was still looking at him when he turned back. "You know, we haven't seen Andy around the house for a few weeks," she said. "Are you sure there's nothing—"

"I'm *fine*, Mom." Two weeks ago Georgie would've given anything for his parents to notice that he'd had a fight with Andy. But now it was too late. There was nothing they could do to help him anymore; he'd been permanently replaced.

She gave his knee another pat. "You know, you can tell me if something's wrong," she said.

"Yep," Georgie said as he opened his door. "I know."

As the orchestra tuned up and practiced, Georgie

sat in the front row of the theater to watch and listen. When they finished, everyone headed backstage, while the ushers began to seat the audience. Georgie spent that time hanging out backstage with the orchestra, listening to them chatter about nothing in particular as they nibbled sandwiches. Georgie ate two ham and cheese sandwiches and a handful of carrots. Then he filed back into the audience and took his usual seat in the front row, smack in the center.

The concert went beautifully. Georgie hummed along softly when he knew the notes, and he watched as all the musicians he had just seen eating turkey sandwiches sat up there on that stage and worked together to play one perfect melody after another.

And after it was all over, when the last notes of music had drifted out of the concert hall, Georgie climbed the steps to the stage. That was one of his favorite things to do—stand up on the stage after everyone in the audience had left and look out onto the rows and rows of empty seats. He liked wandering around all the musicians as they put away their instruments. It was peaceful up there, observing all the things that went on after the concert: the careful cleaning of instruments, the chatting, the discussions about future performances. Georgie was watching one of the musicians put her bassoon back in its case, piece by piece, when Franco, the tuba player, walked right up to him.

"Hey there, Georgie," Franco said, rubbing the shiny bald spot on his head. "How'd you like the show tonight?"

"Went pretty well," Georgie said, nodding. He liked Franco, because sometimes backstage he'd show him card tricks.

"Well, you are our best critic," Franco told him with a wink. "And I hear you're going to be a big brother soon."

Georgie tried not to frown. "Um, yeah," he said.

"Pretty exciting stuff, eh?" He leaned down close toward Georgie, placing his chubby hands on his knees and lowering his voice. "The question around here is what instrument the kid's gonna take up. Personally, I'm betting on the cello, like your old man."

Georgie was sure he was frowning now, but he didn't bother to hide it.

"Some folks swear up and down it'll be the violin, though. You got any guesses, Georgie?"

"Huh?" Georgie looked at Franco and blinked quickly. "No."

Franco straightened up and rubbed his head again. "I gotta say, Georgie, I like the monkey suit."

Georgie looked down at his tux and shrugged. "Mom made me wear it," he answered.

"Well, it looks great," Franco told him. "You look just like one of the band. Ever think of playing tuba?"

Georgie smiled back weakly. "Yeah, maybe," he said. "I . . . uh . . . I think I should go now."

"All right. 'Bye, Georgie. It was good seeing you!"

When Georgie got home, his parents went to change out of their concert clothes right away. But Georgie stayed in his tuxedo, and he did something he hadn't done in a very long time; he sat down at the grand piano in the front room.

He placed himself carefully on the polished black bench, making sure that his custom-made jacket fell *just so* over the edge of the seat. He sat exactly the way he'd seen so many professional pianists sit so many times before—back straight, gaze focused, shoulders squared—and placed his hands on the keys. He spread his fingers as far as he could, farther and farther apart, until the skin between them turned white.

Back when Georgie was five—only eight inches shorter but still big on hope—he used to sit on his mother's lap while she played the piano. He would spread his fingers on top of hers, and their hands would dance through a melody together.

When Georgie was seven—the height of an average three-year-old—he used to tape Popsicle sticks to his fingers before he played. He'd place a phone book on the piano bench and flip through a music book until he found the perfect song, one where the notes moved in great black waves across the page. And then he'd sit there, with his Popsicle-stick fingers, and pretend that he knew how to play it.

But by the time he was nine, Georgie had been to enough of his parents' concerts to understand that no one could play an instrument with Popsicle sticks. And as often as he pushed his ugliest thought to the back of his head, it always managed to find its way out again.

Georgie would never be a musician. He'd never be taller than his dad's cello, let alone able to wrap his arms around it. His feet would never reach the pedals of a piano, and his fingers would never be long enough to play the flute. He'd never be able to grasp a drumstick properly or stretch his arms out far enough to reach the strings of his mother's harp. And if he tried to hold a tuba, it would crush him flat. Even when his parents tried him out on a kid-size violin, Georgie had had trouble bending his wrist to hold the bow. Because he wasn't just short. And he didn't just have stubby fingers. He had back problems and wrist problems, sometimes even trouble bending his elbows all the way. So even if Georgie did have the talent of a violin virtuoso hidden somewhere deep inside him, no one would ever know it.

But the baby? Well, he was practically a professional cellist already, according to Franco. Before Georgie was born, had everyone in the orchestra taken bets on what instrument *he* would play? And how disappointed had they been when they discovered they were wrong? Had his parents been upset too? Georgie couldn't blame them for wanting a second kid—a normal-looking, violin-playing musical genius—but it still hurt, being permanently replaced.

Georgie slammed his fingers into the piano keys as loudly as he could and banged the lid shut. Then he ran to his room and slammed the door too.

He caught sight of the poem on his wall, and suddenly he hated it more than anything in the world.

Choose the instrument that suits you,
Pack your things, and come along.
Everyone is waiting for you—
Only you complete our song.

Georgie didn't belong in this room, this room for *musicians*. He didn't even belong in his own family. He was short, miserable, and still wearing an ugly custom-made tuxedo. He curled up on his bed and buried his head under his pillow so he wouldn't have to see the poem anymore, and he tried as hard as he could to forget about everything, but he simply couldn't. When his parents came in to check on him, Georgie pretended to be asleep.

Then, when the house was completely silent, he crept out of bed in his wrinkled tux and tiptoed into the living room. There, on the couch, he found the big fat book about babies, and he flipped through it until he discovered what he was looking for.

Eleven inches. That's how tall the baby was now. Georgie returned to his room, made the mark on his closet wall, changed into his pajamas, and then climbed into bed. But he didn't sleep very well. He couldn't stop thinking about how *eleven inches* was almost as tall as the violin he'd been completely unable to play.

Five weeks later, on a Thursday afternoon just before school let out, Georgie sat at his desk with his chin in his hands. He watched as, three rows up and two seats over, Andy struck his pencil on the floor twice. And he watched as Russ crossed the room to use the pencil sharpener, then passed Andy's desk on his way back, grabbing a note as he walked by.

Basically, Georgie realized, his life was pretty much over. He had zero friends, Baby Godzilla was now 14.4 inches tall, and his parents were still acting like baby-loving idiots. Soon enough Andy would move, he'd no longer be just six blocks away, and that would be it for their friendship—no chance of recovery. The only good thing in the world was that tomorrow was the last day Georgie would ever have to spend working with Jeanie the Meanie on their Abraham Lincoln project.

For four whole Fridays Georgie had done his best to ignore Jeanie while they worked on their project together. Two weeks in a row he'd told Mr. Myers he needed to do more research in the library, because only one person was allowed to have a hall pass at a time. The next week he figured he'd done enough research, so he went into the boys' bathroom and stayed there for twenty minutes. And the week after that he told Mr. Myers he thought he had the flu and stayed in the nurse's office until she told him his temperature was perfectly normal and kicked him out.

It wasn't like he hadn't been doing any work on the project. He had. Just not with Jeanie. And that was fine by him.

Mr. Myers had given every pair of partners a piece of paper to fill out, which they had to turn in with their report, and it was supposed to guarantee that each person had done equal work. So far, Georgie and Jeanie's paper looked like this:

I, _Georgie Bishop_, worked on the
following parts of my project individually:

1. The Civil War

2. The Emancipation Proclamation

3. Abraham Lincoln's reelection

I, _Jeanette Ann Wallace_ ∧ the first, worked on the
following parts of my project individually:

1. How when Abe Lincoln was a kid he lived in a log cabin.

2. How his mom died when he was very young.

3. How he was not very good at owning a grocery store.

We worked on the following parts of our
project together:

1.

2.

3.

X _____   X _____

Signature   Signature

Georgie figured that tomorrow they'd work together and look up some stuff about the Gettysburg Address. Then they could fill in the last three blanks. He wasn't looking forward to it, but it had to be done.

Three minutes before the bell rang, Mr. Myers cleared his throat.

"I want to remind you all," he said, "that your president projects are due first thing tomorrow morning. And don't forget to sign off on everything you've worked on."

Georgie raised his hand high.

"Yes, Georgie?"

"Um, don't you mean they're due tomorrow *afternoon*?" Georgie asked.

Mr. Myers frowned. "No," he replied. "Tomorrow morning. First thing."

Georgie raised his hand again. "But don't we get time in class to work on them?"

"No," Mr. Myers said.

"But we're not done yet."

"Georgie, if you look at the handout I gave you

when we started this project, you'll see that the due date is marked very clearly. If you haven't finished yet, I suggest you and your partner get together tonight to work on it."

"But—"

"Tomorrow morning. No exceptions."

Georgie was pretty sure he could see Andy laughing at him at the front of the room, but he had bigger things to worry about. *Get together with Jeanie the Meanie after school?*

When the bell rang, Georgie turned around and shoved the piece of paper they had to sign under Jeanie's nose. "Here," he said. "Sign this. I'll finish the report tonight and fill in all the blanks."

Jeanie pushed the paper away and picked up her backpack. "No way," she said.

"*Jeanie,*" Georgie growled at her, "*I'm* going to do all the work. You just have to say you helped."

She tilted her head to look at him sideways. "For someone with a fat head," she said, "your brain's pretty puny." She yanked at his arm and began writing

115

on it. "I'm not gonna *lie*," she told him while she wrote. "We're supposed to work together." She shoved his arm back. "That's where I live," she said, pointing at the scribble on his arm. "Be there at six, fathead." And she left the classroom.

At six o'clock Georgie's dad dropped him off in front of Jeanie the Meanie's house. "You know, Georgie," his father said as Georgie opened the car door, "I think it's great you're making new friends."

"Yeah," Georgie said. "Great." He shut the door and waved as his dad drove off.

Seconds after Georgie rang the doorbell, Jeanie pulled him into the house. Then she led him quickly up the stairs to her room, passing her family at top speed. "That's my dad, that's my brother, that's my brother," she told Georgie as they scurried past. "This is Georgie." The Meanie family hardly looked up.

She pushed him into her room and closed the door,

then plopped herself down on her bed. Georgie looked around for a place to sit, but the desk chair was heaped with clothes, and the only other spot was next to Jeanie on the bed. Georgie sat down on the floor.

He unzipped his backpack and pulled out his books. "Let's just get this done fast, all right?" he said.

"Fine," Jeanie replied. She got out her own books and flipped through them. "What are we looking for?"

Georgie closed his eyes for a moment, like his dad did when he was trying to stay calm. He didn't want to get into a fight with Jeanie the Meanie in her own home. He just wanted to finish the report and leave as quickly as possible. "The Gettysburg Address," he said through clenched teeth.

"Oh, yeah."

They had been quiet for about two minutes when Jeanie said, "Are you gonna sign up to be one of the presidents in the play?"

Georgie tried to ignore her and keep reading, but she threw a stuffed chicken at him and he looked up. Jeanie smiled and acted like they were already in the middle of a conversation. "So are you?"

Georgie kicked the chicken across the floor. "No," he said, and he kept reading.

"Well, I am."

Georgie ignored her.

This time she threw a stuffed armadillo. "I'm going to be in the play," she told him when he looked up.

Georgie took a long, deep breath. Obviously, there was no way to ignore Jeanie the Meanie when she wanted to talk about something. "Who are you going to sign up for?" he asked her, even though he didn't care.

She shrugged like she really wasn't interested in talking. "Herbert Hoover," she said.

"What?" He put his book down. "How come *Herbert Hoover*?" Anyone with half a brain would pick George Washington.

"'Cause he was really cool," Jeanie said. She sounded excited now. "I looked stuff up about him in the library. He was a millionaire, for one thing. Plus his parents died when he was just a kid, and he lived with his uncle. And he helped build the *Hoover Dam*."

She raised her eyebrows at Georgie when she said that, like Georgie would jump up and squeal, "Ooh, really? The Hoover Dam?" But he didn't.

"And," she continued, "he was president during the Great Depression. That's a lot of drama. It's the perfect acting role."

"Oh, okay," Georgie said, and turned back to his book. What he really wanted to know was why Jeanie could spend so much time looking up information about a president they didn't even have to do a report on, but reading four words about the Gettysburg Address was impossible.

"I'm gonna be an actress, you know," Jeanie told him.

Georgie just nodded and kept reading.

"Or a writer," she went on. "Or an obstetrician. That's a doctor who delivers babies."

Georgie puffed out his cheeks. The last thing he needed to hear about was *babies*. "I'm trying to read," he said.

Jeanie shook her head like Georgie was the crazy one, but she started reading too. Not for long, though.

"So how come you're not going to sign up to be a president?" she asked him.

He glared at her. "I don't want to."

"You don't like acting?"

He turned a page and didn't answer.

"Do you get stage fright? Some people get stage fright. Do you get it real bad, like where you have to throw up? I don't get it at all."

"Okay."

Jeanie stared at him a little longer, and Georgie continued to ignore her until she picked up one of her books. "Hey, here's something," she said. "Did you know Lincoln was the tallest president there ever was? He was six foot four."

Georgie was losing his patience. "Jeanie, we have to write about the Gettysburg Address, not how tall the president was."

"Oh." She nodded like that had just occurred to her. She was silent a few moments more until . . . "Hey, did you know the Gettysburg Address wasn't an address at all? It was a *speech*."

Georgie couldn't take it anymore. "Yeah, I knew

121

that," he said. "I knew that six weeks ago. It's a *big* speech, and we're supposed to write about it."

"Oh," she said, shrugging. "Well, I thought it was an address." She plucked a pen off her bed and began to write in the book.

"What are you doing?" Georgie asked her. "You can't do that! It's a library book!"

"Well, it's confusing," Jeanie said. "And I'm fixing it, so the next person who reads it will know what it means."

Georgie shook his head and went back to his book. But he hadn't been reading long before he was hit in the head by a stuffed otter.

"Hey!" Georgie cried, rubbing his ear.

"Did you know my mom sang backup for Mary Ann LeBaz for a whole year?" Jeanie asked. "She even went on tour."

"Um . . ." Georgie had no idea who Mary Ann LeBaz was, and he didn't care.

"You wanna see a picture of her?"

"Not really. I'd rather—"

"Look." Jeanie pointed to a faded photo taped

above her bed. "That's my mom."

Georgie glanced at it briefly. "Wow. That's great. Now can we—"

"I didn't know her, though. She died when I was really little." She turned to Georgie. "Are *your* parents dead?" she asked him.

"Huh? No."

"Oh. That's cool."

Georgie suddenly got the feeling he was going to be there forever, trapped in Jeanie the Meanie's room, listening to her talk about Herbert Hoover and her dead mom until the end of time.

"Um, Jeanie?" Georgie said. "Can we, um, actually start working on the Gettysburg Address now?"

"What do you think we've been doing?" Jeanie said. "Here." She passed him her book. "I think this is some pretty good stuff."

Georgie looked at the page. It *did* look helpful. It was Abraham Lincoln's entire speech written out, word for word. Georgie began to read. After a minute or two he looked up. "What's 'consecrate' mean?" he asked.

Jeanie shrugged. She was staring at the picture on her wall again. "I dunno," she said.

"Well, do you think we could look it up or something? It's important."

She pointed to a shelf on the wall above her dresser. "There's a dictionary up there."

Georgie looked up at the shelf. "Can, um, can *you* get it?" he asked Jeanie.

She blinked at him. "Why?" she said. "You're the one who wants to know so bad."

"Yeah, but . . ." Georgie hated to say it. "It's really high up."

"So use the chair," Jeanie said.

Georgie closed his book with a thud and stood up. He pushed all the clothes off the desk chair onto the floor and then dragged the chair over to the dresser. He climbed on top and stretched until he finally reached the dictionary.

After he'd looked up *consecrate*, the speech made a little more sense. Now they just had to write about it. But that was pretty hard when Jeanie would not stop talking.

"You know my brother Victor? You saw him down-stairs. He was the one with the bad hairdo. Not the one with the *really* bad hairdo, that was Mike. Well, he has this hamster, only it—"

"Jeanie, can we just write this, please?"

"Yeah, yeah," she said. "Sheesh."

But two minutes later she was talking again. "You know, I really think you should sign up for the play. And you know who I think you should be? *George Washington.*"

Georgie blinked. "What did you say?"

"Nothing." She smiled and returned to her piece of paper.

She couldn't know, Georgie decided. There was no way. She was probably just making stuff up. He'd have to ignore her.

But he couldn't.

"Why'd you say that?" he asked. "That thing about George Washington?"

Jeanie tapped her paper with a pencil. "Are your parents short like you?" she asked. "Or are they tall, like regular people? 'Cause I was reading this book in the library, and it said that most people like you have regular—"

He threw the armadillo at her.

"Can we finish already?" Georgie said. "I want to get home before I turn eighty."

Jeanie picked up her armadillo and petted its head. And after that, even though Georgie couldn't believe it, she didn't talk about anything but Abraham Lincoln for over an hour.

At last they were almost done. Almost.

"We need a last sentence," Jeanie said, staring at the paper.

"How 'bout 'The End'?" Georgie mumbled. He just wanted to go home.

"No," she said. "It has to be something that shows we learned a lot."

Georgie sighed. "How about 'And that is why Abraham Lincoln was the best president the United States has ever had'?" Georgie didn't think that was true at all, because obviously George Washington was a *way* better president. Washington was a Founding

Father, for crying out loud. But the sentence definitely made their report sound like it was over, and if it was over, Georgie could go home.

"Perfect," Jeanie said, and she wrote it down.

Georgie called his dad to pick him up, and even though he told Jeanie she really, *really* didn't have to, she waited with him by the front door. She kept staring at him, her head tilted to the side.

"So?" she said after a good five minutes of staring. "Are you gonna sign up to be George Washington? Or are you too scared?"

Georgie played with the zipper on his jacket. "I don't know why you keep talking about George Washington," he said, trying to sound convincing.

Her smile was huge now. "I told you I'd figure it out," she said.

"How did you—"

But Georgie didn't get to finish his question. All of a sudden he heard a voice from the other end of the hallway. "Hey, Rat Eater!" someone hollered. Georgie swiveled around and saw one of Jeanie's older brothers, leaning against the wall with his arms crossed. "Who's your boyfriend?" he asked Jeanie.

"Shove it, Fart Face!" Jeanie shouted back.

"Nice comeback, Broccoli For Brains."

"Go away, Mike."

Mike grinned. "Why? You want some alone time with your boyfriend? You gonna kiss him? Hey, Victor!" Mike called into the living room. "Come here! Puke Breath's gonna kiss her boyfriend!"

"Shut up, loser!" Jeanie screeched back.

Victor came into the hallway then. "What's all the noise for, Puss Head?" he asked Jeanie. "You and your boyfriend break up?"

Georgie could feel his face getting hot. Why did he have to be stuck here, in this horrible house? "I'm not her boyfriend!" he shouted.

Victor and Mike were as calm as ever. "Well, that's not too surprising," Mike said with a shrug. "Who would want to go out with someone like Skunk Feet?" He turned to Victor. "Who would even be *friends* with Skunk Feet?"

Jeanie put her hands on her hips. "Shut *up*, Mike."

"Oh, that's right," Mike went on. "I forgot. You don't *have* any friends, do you, Elephant Nose?"

"I do too have friends!" Jeanie bellowed.

"Oh, yeah?" Victor jumped in. "Name one."

Jeanie just stood there, and Mike grinned.

"I bet this kid's not even your friend." Mike pointed to Georgie. "Are you?"

Georgie looked at Jeanie. Her mouth was creased in an angry frown, and she was staring at him, waiting for his response. Georgie turned to Mike and Victor. They were waiting too. He just wouldn't say anything, he decided. That was the safest bet.

"Thought so," Mike said with a laugh. He and Victor went back to the living room.

Out the window Georgie saw his dad's car turn the corner. He pushed open the door and raced outside, but Jeanie followed him. She grabbed hold of his arm and held on hard.

"You know what?" she told him. She was *mad*. Fuming. "I *used* to feel sorry for you. But it turns out you're just mean!" And she let him go with a shove.

But just before Georgie got to his dad's car, Jeanie shouted at him again. "Hey!" she bellowed. "Hey, George *Washington*!" He turned. "The reason I know about your stupid president middle name," she hollered, "is that it's in the roll book, you slug face!" And she slammed her front door.

Time for another favor. I want you to open your mouth as wide as you can. Now grab your tongue between your thumb and pointer finger and hold on to it for a few seconds.

Keep holding.

You notice how your fingers are getting all wet and slobbery like that? Notice how your tongue is starting to feel dry, how every time you take a breath, your tongue gets a little bit colder? You probably think that's what happens to everyone when they grab their tongue. I bet you think it's no big deal at all, that anyone can pinch their tongue like that.

Well, Georgie can too.

I just thought you should know that, that Georgie can do a bunch of stuff, same as you. Even dumb stuff like grabbing his tongue. He doesn't do it a lot, but he could if he wanted to. He wouldn't even think twice about it.

You can let go of your tongue now. You might want to dry your fingers off before you turn the page, though.

As soon as the bell rang the next morning, Mr. Myers collected their reports. Georgie looked at the red folder with the picture of the top hat glued to the front before he handed it in. Finally over. No more Jeanie the Meanie, ever again.

Tap-tap-tap.

Georgie swiveled around.

"Why don't you hand in our report before we fail already?" Jeanie asked him.

After Mr. Myers had collected all the reports, he passed out pieces of paper and said that everyone who wanted to be in the play had to write down their name and the president they wanted to be. Mr. Myers said he would collect all the papers and make his decision before the end of the day.

Georgie stared at his piece of paper long and hard, his pencil poised above it. "George Washington," his brain told his hand. "Write down George Washington." But the pencil wasn't moving.

Jeanie poked him in the back. "Why aren't you writing anything, Donkey Breath?" she asked him, her head peeking over his shoulder. "You *do* have stage fright."

Georgie quickly crumpled up his paper. "I do not," he said. "Leave me alone."

As everyone else's pencils scratched across their papers, Georgie sat with his chin in his hands, his empty piece of paper scrunched into a ball, and watched Andy chew on his pencil at the front of the room. He wondered where Andy would move to in the summer. Would his family find a bigger house in the same neighborhood, or would it be far away? Would Andy switch schools? Georgie wished he could just ask him.

By the time the class came back from lunch, Mr.

Myers had posted the cast of characters for the play. Everyone raced to the wall to read it. Georgie knew he probably shouldn't even look, but he was dying to see who would play George Washington. Finally he wiggled his way to the front of the crowd.

Russ Wilkins. Of course. *Russ Wilkins* was going to be George Washington. Well, at least he wouldn't have to powder his hair.

Georgie was turning to go back to his seat when something caught his eye. His name was on the list too.

Right next to Abraham Lincoln.

There had to be some mistake.

Georgie pushed his way through his classmates and rushed to Mr. Myers's desk.

"Mr. Myers," Georgie said, trying not to appear frantic, "why did you put me down for Abraham Lincoln?"

Mr. Myers set down a stack of papers. "Because you signed up for it," he replied.

"But . . . but . . ." Georgie stammered. "No, I didn't. I don't want—"

"You know, Georgie," Mr. Myers began, gesturing

with his pencil, "there were a lot of kids who wanted that part. But I was so happy when I saw *your* name. I think this will be really good for you. And I have to say, from what I read of your report at lunch, it seemed really inspired. I know you'll make a fantastic president."

"But, Mr. My—"

"You can't back out now, Georgie. I'll be so disappointed."

Georgie shuffled back to his seat. *Abraham Lincoln?* The tallest president ever? How could Georgie possibly get up in front of a huge room full of people and pretend to be *tall*? He'd be laughed right off the stage.

Jeanie the Meanie caught Georgie's eye just before he slipped into his seat. She smiled, looking meaner than ever. "Guess it's a good thing you don't have stage fright, huh?" she said.

Georgie was going to kill her.

Georgie didn't want to tell his parents about his part in the play right away. In fact, he didn't want to tell them *ever*. He didn't think they needed to be there to witness their son die of embarrassment.

But the next Friday afternoon a letter came in the mail about practice and the need to rehearse lines, and just as Georgie had feared, his parents were thrilled.

"I think this could be good for you, Georgie," his mom told him. Why did everyone keep saying that?

"Abe Lincoln was an excellent president," his dad added. "One of the finest."

Georgie wanted to mention to them that—just in case they were wondering—Abe Lincoln had also been six feet four, *not* forty-two inches. But Georgie didn't say one word about it, because he knew that the second he did, his mom and dad would tell him something stupid and parenty, like it didn't matter what he looked like as long as he portrayed the spirit of a president and kept a positive attitude.

Well, that was garbage, and Georgie knew it. The truth was, no matter how positive his attitude, once he stepped onto the stage in the gym and announced, "Hello, my name is Abraham Lincoln," everyone was going to laugh. *Everyone.* Even the adults would laugh. A dwarf playing Abraham Lincoln? They were going to *explode* with laughter.

At least Georgie could take his mind off things for a little while that weekend. His mom had signed him up for swimming lessons at the public pool a few weeks before, and Saturday was his very first day.

Georgie was actually sort of excited about the lessons. He was already a pretty good swimmer, and maybe if he took lessons, he could be *really* good. Swimming wasn't hard on his back like running was. When he used to race Andy in laps across the pool, sometimes Georgie even won. He knew he'd never be in the Olympics or anything, but he figured it would be nice to have a sport he was good at.

And today it was warm out, really warm, for the first time in ages. It was like the sun had been tricked into thinking it was already spring. It was a perfect day for the pool, Georgie thought. He only hoped that everyone in the world wouldn't be there.

When they arrived, though, Georgie was relieved to see that one of the two indoor pools had been marked off just for lessons. Everyone else was splashing around in the free-swim pool, and they looked like they were having too much fun to pay attention to the swim lesson kids.

Georgie went into the bathroom and changed into his baggy red swim trunks. When he came back out, he stopped for a moment to look at his mom, who was sitting in a folding chair by the side of the pool. Her stomach had been getting big lately. Last night, when she was practicing for a concert, Georgie had noticed that she'd had to shift around in her chair a bit before she found a comfortable spot between her belly and the harp.

She flipped a page in her magazine as Georgie set his clothes on the table beside her. "You all ready?" she asked.

"Yep."

Georgie met his swimming teacher, whose name was Kimberly, and hopped into the pool to start his lesson. Right away Georgie was glad he had his own private teacher. The kids in the kindergarten swim class couldn't stop staring at him, so Kimberly led him to the other side of the pool to practice in peace.

He was getting the hang of things pretty quickly. Kimberly said he had great kicks, and even though he had some trouble floating because he couldn't stretch his arms out very far, he knew he was doing well all around.

Five minutes before Georgie's lesson was over, as he was coming up for air after a lap across the pool, he caught sight of a flash of bright red hair.

Allison Housman!

She was stepping out of the bathroom with one of her friends. A towel, stamped with cheerful green frogs on lily pads, was draped over her shoulders. Georgie's ears cleared up just in time to hear her laugh. The sound echoed off the walls, and he watched as her sandals flip-flip-flopped to the edge of the free-swim pool.

"Georgie?" Kimberly was calling him.

He turned. "Huh?"

"That was great! Didn't you think so?"

He tried to shake Allison and her frog towel out of his head. "Um, yeah," he said.

"Okay, I'd like you to do five more laps, exactly like that one, and then we can call it a day. Remember to stretch your arms."

Georgie did his laps, but he wasn't concentrating. Every time his arm sliced through the water, it slapped onto the surface of the pool with an *Allison, Allison*. And the splash of his kicks sounded suspiciously like *Housman Housman Housman Housman*. Georgie was sure everyone could hear it echoing through the whole room. He tried to make his kicks softer, but Kimberly hollered at him that he was losing his form.

When Georgie finished his laps, Kimberly congratulated him on a fine first lesson and told his mom that he was an excellent swimmer. Georgie's mom beamed as Kimberly left.

"Awesome job, G!" she told him. She bent over the side of the pool, where Georgie was hanging on. "Do you like your teacher?"

"Yeah, she's cool," Georgie answered. "Hey, Mom, can we stay for a while? I want to go swimming some more in, um, in the free-swim pool."

"Oh, Georgie, I have to go. I'm sorry, hon. I have a piano lesson."

Georgie watched as drips of water fell from his arm onto the tile. "But I really want to stay, Mom," he said. He was doing his best to look pitiful. "I haven't even gotten to swim for fun yet."

"That's true, but—"

"I could walk home."

"I don't know, G—"

"Mom, it's only twelve blocks. I've walked home tons of times without you."

She looked up, trying to decide. "Never by yourself, though. You were always with Andy or someone."

"I'll be *fine*, Mom."

She took a deep breath in and then finally let it out.

"All right. But only for an hour, okay? Come straight home afterward. And don't talk to strangers. And don't—"

"*Mom.*"

"All right, all right." She kissed the top of his head. "I'll see you at home."

"'Bye, Mom."

As soon as his mother left, Georgie climbed up the metal ladder and padded his way to the other pool, his swimming trunks dripping a trail of water behind him. He found Allison and her friend stretched out in two plastic lawn chairs. They were reading a magazine together and giggling. Allison saw Georgie and waved to him.

"Hey, Georgie!" she called.

He came closer, trying to look cool. But he knew he just looked like himself. "Um, hi," he said.

Allison smiled, and Georgie noticed she had absolutely perfect teeth. "This is Nicki," she told him, pointing to her friend.

"Hi," he mumbled, but he didn't really look at her.

Nicki sat up. "Hey, you're that kid," she said.

142

"Huh?" Georgie asked.

Allison poked Nicki in the side with her elbow. "Georgie's mom's my piano teacher," she told her friend.

"Oh," Nicki said. She nodded. "Well, that's nice." Her voice was high. Too high, like she was talking to a four-year-old.

Georgie looked down at the ground and shuffled his feet. Then he looked back at Allison, who gave him a friendly smile but didn't say anything. Nicki only stared at him. Georgie scratched his head, just to have something to do, and looked back down at his feet. His trunks were still dripping water. The puddle that surrounded him was inching its way toward Allison's frog towel, neatly folded on the ground beside her chair. If he stood there any longer, her towel would be soaked. And then she'd *hate* him. He had to get out of there.

"Um," Georgie said, rubbing his elbow, "I'm gonna go swim now."

"Oh, okay," Allison said with a smile. "Have fun."

Georgie slumped off to the pool steps. As he walked

away, he heard Nicki whisper, "I didn't know you knew *that* kid."

Georgie slid into the pool and let the warm water envelop him. He ducked his head underwater and stayed down as long as he possibly could, with his eyes squeezed shut and his cheeks puffed out. When he finally came up for air, he kept his eyes closed so all the water would drip off before he opened them. And he was standing like that, up to his chin in the shallow end of the pool with his eyes still closed, when he heard the twang of the diving board and a splash as someone hit the water.

When he opened his eyes, Georgie found Jeanie the Meanie barreling toward him at full force.

"You know, George Washington"—Jeanie snickered when she reached his end of the pool—"there's no way that redheaded girl is ever going to fall in love with you."

No matter what Georgie did, Jeanie would simply not leave him alone. When he tried to swim laps, she swam behind him the whole time, shouting at him in between gulps of air and splashing him with water. When he circled somersaults in the shallow end of the pool, she was right beside him, standing on her head and kicking him in the shoulder when she fell over. When he climbed the diving board, she followed him up the steps. And when he paused for a second before his dive, just to see if Allison was watching him, Jeanie hollered at him to "stop being such a fraidy cat and get diving already!" That made him so mad that when he jumped, Georgie fell into the water with a splat, his body splayed out flat as a board, so that the water stung like pinpricks all over. And worst of all, Allison *had* been watching.

Jeanie ran off the board at full speed and landed in an impressive cannonball. When she came back up for air, she wiped her wet bangs from her forehead and was just starting to splash Georgie's way when the lifeguard blew his whistle at her and made her get out of the pool for a lecture about running. Georgie laughed out loud, and Jeanie narrowed her eyes at him from across the water.

Finally free from Jeanie the Meanie, Georgie decided to do laps across the pool. Really fast laps. Butterfly strokes. Maybe Allison would see him and be impressed and think, *Wow, I can't do the butterfly stroke like that. That's cool.* Maybe. But then . . . Where *was* Allison anyway?

She was gone! Her friend too! And her frog towel! Gone, gone, gone. She'd left without even saying good-bye.

Georgie swam to the shallow end of the pool and climbed out. Then he grabbed his clothes and raced to go change in the boys' bathroom. He was still a little wet when he came out, but he didn't care. He didn't want to stay there a second longer.

His sneakers squished in the small puddles of water as he left the pool and stepped outside. He wished he hadn't stayed after his mom had left. He wasn't looking forward to walking all the way home with his soggy swim trunks wrapped in his towel. It was getting colder by the minute. At least it was only twelve blocks.

Georgie was just crossing the parking lot when he heard Jeanie the Meanie shouting behind him. "Hey!" she hollered. "Where do you think you're going?"

Georgie spun around on his heel. *"Home,"* he said.

"Me too. Don't follow me." Jeanie was still wearing her bathing suit. She wasn't holding any clothes or even a towel. Just her bathing suit and flip-flops.

Georgie wanted to ask why she didn't have anything with her if she was so ready to go home, but he didn't. *"You* don't follow *me,"* he told her.

"I'll follow you if I want," she said. And she did, one step behind him the whole way. She was singing songs under her breath, and even though Georgie couldn't hear any of the words, he had a feeling they weren't very nice.

On and on they walked, house after house, block after block, and Georgie started to wonder if Jeanie was going to follow him straight through his doorway. But then they reached Andy's house, and Georgie stopped thinking about Jeanie the Meanie.

There was no bike in Andy's driveway. Andy was probably out somewhere, having fun without him. With Russ, most likely.

Jeanie interrupted his thoughts. "Whatcha looking at, Hippo Face? Why'd you stop walking?"

Georgie realized that he had, in fact, stopped walking.

"Whose house is this?" Jeanie asked.

"No one's," Georgie said quickly. "I don't even know them."

But Jeanie wasn't listening. Georgie followed her gaze to the mailbox. *Moretti* was painted on the side in scrolling red letters.

"This is Andy's house, isn't it?" she asked.

"No," Georgie said.

"Yes, it is." She crossed the lawn and tried to peer through the window. "We should say hi."

"I don't think anyone's home," Georgie said. "Come on, Jeanie! You can't look in their windows."

"It's not like I can see anything anyway. Stupid curtain." She turned around, and Georgie glared at her. "I just wanted to *look*. Jeez, I'm not stealing anything." She moved to the next window.

"Will you *stop*!" Georgie cried. "Come on!"

"How come you don't ever hang out with Andy anymore anyway?" Jeanie asked as she peered through a crack in the curtain. "Did you guys get in a fight?"

"No. We're just not friends anymore." Georgie didn't know why he was still talking to her. He should just walk away and go home. But he couldn't leave Jeanie the Meanie at Andy's house by herself. What if she opened the door and walked right in? "You'd really better stop doing that," he told her.

Jeanie ignored him. "You know what we should do?" she asked. "'Cause he stopped being friends with you? We should break his windows."

"What? No! You're crazy."

"Why not? If you hate him." Jeanie walked across the lawn and picked up a medium-size rock. "Come on, throw this one."

Georgie was still standing on the sidewalk. "No! I'm not gonna break his windows. That's the dumbest thing I ever heard of. Anyway, I don't hate him."

"How come? I would. And I'd break his windows too."

Georgie snorted. "No wonder they call you Jeanie the Meanie," he said.

That's when she threw the rock. But not at the house. Jeanie threw the rock at *Georgie*. And she hit him in the leg.

"Ow!" Georgie cried. It really hurt. It was even bleeding a little.

"Don't *ever* call me that!" Jeanie bellowed. "Ever!" She picked up another rock and lifted it over her head, but before she could throw it, they heard a screen door slam, and Jeanie whirled around.

Nonna Rosa was standing in the doorway in her slippers, a puzzled expression on her face.

"Giorgino!" Nonna Rosa cried. Then she said a

whole bunch of other stuff Georgie couldn't understand at all, except for *bambini*, which he was pretty sure meant "children," and she said Andrea a few times, and once he thought she might have said Russ, but he could have been wrong. She spoke very quickly, her eyes darting back and forth between Georgie's bloody leg and Jeanie, who had hidden her rock behind her back and was now smiling innocently. Then all at once she stepped into the house, leaving the door open.

Jeanie raced over to him. "I'm getting out of here, *quick*," she said, "before she calls the cops or something."

"The cops!" Georgie cried. "Why would she do that?"

"Hello! 'Cause we were, like, on her property, attacking each other."

"*I* wasn't attacking anyone," Georgie said. "If anyone's going to jail, it's you."

"What!" Jeanie shouted. "You were the one who—"

Nonna Rosa stepped out of the house once more.

She was wearing her coat, but she still had slippers on her feet. She held up a pair of keys and pointed to the car.

"What's going on?" Jeanie whispered.

"I—I don't know."

Nonna Rosa started talking again, quick streams of words that didn't make any sense at all. Georgie strained his ears to hear something, *anything*, that he understood.

Casa. He caught the word *casa.* Or at least he thought he did.

"House," he told Jeanie. "I think she said house. Or home. Something like that."

"So?" Jeanie asked.

"So I think she wants to drive us home."

"Why would she do that?"

Georgie shrugged. "I dunno. Probably so we won't stand around in her yard and throw rocks at each other."

"Oh."

Nonna Rosa ushered them into the car. Georgie sat in the front seat, and Jeanie plopped herself in the back, suddenly cheerful again.

They pulled out of the driveway, and Jeanie tapped Georgie on the shoulder. "What language does she speak?" she asked him.

"Italian."

"Really! I know some Italian too. I know an Italian opera." She sat up straight in her seat and began to sing, "La dawn ay MOW bee lay! La dawn ay MOW bee lay!"

Nonna Rosa smiled as she turned a corner. *"Brava!"* she said. *"Brava, ragazza!"*

Jeanie stopped singing. "What'd she say?" she asked Georgie.

"I dunno," he said. *"You're* the one who speaks Italian."

Jeanie stuck out her tongue and turned to look out the window, arms folded across her chest.

Georgie jumped in his seat when he saw his house rush past the window. "Um, Nonna Rosa?" he said. "We passed my house."

"Che dici, Giorgino?"

"What?" Georgie asked her. "We passed my house.

That's my house back there, Nonna Rosa." He pointed at it, but Nonna Rosa just smiled and nodded. She clearly didn't understand. *"Casa,"* he said. *"Casa.* My *casa."*

"Sì," she said with a nod. That meant "yes," Georgie knew that much. But he had no idea what she said next.

"What?" he asked again. "I don't understand." Nonna Rosa repeated herself, but Georgie still didn't know what she was saying. *"What?"*

He strained his ears again, and finally he caught something he understood. Two words this time, right next to each other. *Casa* and then *Russ.*

"Oh, no," Georgie said. He turned around in his seat to look at Jeanie. "I think she's taking us to Russ's house." Jeanie continued to stare out the window without saying anything. "I think that's where Andy is maybe. And she thought we came to see him, so she's taking us to Russ's."

Jeanie still didn't say anything, so Georgie turned back around. This was horrible. The worst. How was he going to explain things to Andy when he showed up at Russ's house? And with Jeanie the Meanie, to boot.

"Nonna Rosa," he said, "I don't want to go to Russ's house. I just want to go home." He pointed out the window again, but she just nodded and smiled.

Georgie figured once they got to Russ's house, at least he could call his mom and have her pick him up. That is, if he lived through the embarrassment of showing up at the house of the best friend of *his* ex-best friend with someone else's grandmother and the meanest girl alive wearing nothing but her bathing suit. They'd think he was crazy, or worse, that he'd gone there on *purpose*, to try to be friends with Andy again. And Andy would say how much he hated him, in front of everybody—Russ and Jeanie the Meanie, who would of course tell the entire school on Monday—and *then* Georgie would have to ask to please use Russ's phone so his mommy could come get him. No, this definitely wasn't good.

But as much as Georgie wasn't looking forward to going to Russ's house, he did start to wonder if they would *ever* get there. He hadn't realized that Russ lived so far away. Nonna Rosa just kept driving and driving, and even though Georgie didn't know exactly what time they had gotten into the car, it sure felt like a while ago. He started to watch the clock. Five minutes passed. Then ten. Then fifteen. Nonna Rosa started muttering to herself. She looked confused.

"Nonna Rosa?" Georgie asked quietly. "Are we lost?"

"Lost?" The way she repeated the word, with extra emphasis on the *t*, made it sound funny. She looked at him with raised eyebrows. *"Lost?"* she said again.

Georgie nodded. "Yeah, you know, *lost*. Are we lost?" He found a map in the pocket of his door and pulled it out, showing it to her. Then he unfolded half of it and traced one of the street lines with his finger. "Are we"—he let his finger follow a street all the way off the map, and then he spun it in circles a few times—*"lost?"*

"Ah." Nonna Rosa pinched her lips together and nodded down at him. *"Sì,"* she said, looking quite worried indeed. *"Siamo 'lost.'"*

Of all the places they could have been lost in, Georgie figured this was probably the worst. There were no houses around, or gas stations, or stores, nowhere they could actually ask someone for directions. Instead there were trees. Trees and dirt. And still Nonna Rosa kept driving.

Georgie looked at the map in his hand to try to figure out where they were and then realized it was a map of Iowa. *That* wasn't going to help any.

He turned around and found Jeanie curled up with her feet on the seat, still staring out the window. Georgie almost felt sorry for her, with nothing but her tattered blue bathing suit on. And was she *shivering*? The skin around her knuckles was purple, and there were tiny goose bumps all up and down her arms.

"Jeanie," Georgie said softly, "um, I think we're lost."

Jeanie's ponytail, off-center as always, was drooping heavily. A drop of water fell from the tips of her hair and landed on her bathing suit, where it promptly disappeared into the fabric. "I hate you" was all she said.

"What?" he cried. Georgie couldn't believe this. He was lost, and he kind of had to pee, and he'd actually felt *sorry* for Jeanie the Meanie for an entire second. "Why do you hate *me*?"

She stared out the window while she spoke. "I'm being kidnapped by some old Italian lady and a dwarf, and I'll *never* get home, and my dad'll think I was *murdered*—" She stopped talking and wiped at her eyes with the back of her hand.

"Well, I'm lost too," Georgie said. "Maybe if you'd stop *crying* for three seconds and help me figure out where we are, we could get home."

She punched him through the seat.

"Ow!" he cried. "What's the matter with you?"

"I *hate* you!" she hollered.

"*Bambini!*" Nonna Rosa brought the car to a screeching halt in the middle of the road, and Georgie opened his door and hopped out right there. He couldn't stay in the car one second longer with Jeanie the Meanie. He noticed a convenience store not too far away. He'd walk there and see if they had a pay phone so he could call his parents.

Georgie started walking, and Nonna Rosa drove behind him slowly, calling to him through the open window. But he didn't care how many times she called him *Giorgino*. *Little Georgie*. There was no way he was getting back in that car.

As Georgie got closer to the store, he realized that it was closed. *Great*, he thought. But there was a pay phone outside. That was something at least. He'd be able to call his parents and get out of there.

Nonna Rosa parked by the side of the road, and Georgie stormed right up to the pay phone. He had some coins in his pocket.

But as soon as Georgie reached up to put the change in the coin slot, he realized he had a problem. He wasn't tall enough to use the phone. Not even close. He looked all around him, but there was nothing he could stand on. No crate, or phone book, not even a cardboard box.

He stomped over to the car and found Nonna Rosa hunched over the hood, vigorously studying the map of Iowa. Georgie didn't even know how to begin explaining to her that that wasn't going to help them, so he tapped on Jeanie's window.

"*What?*" Jeanie hollered through the glass. She was crying pretty hard now.

"I need help," he told her.

She shook her head at him, her eyes full of tears.

"Look!" he cried. "We're not ever gonna get home unless you help me! We'll be stuck out here forever!"

Jeanie turned her back to him and wrapped her arms around her knees, rocking back and forth.

"Jeanie!" Georgie rapped on the window. "Come on, Jeanie! I need your help! Come *on*!" He tried to open her door, but she turned around quickly and locked it, and all the other doors with it. Nonna Rosa looked up and muttered something, and Georgie just shrugged at her. *Now* what was he going to do?

He walked back to the pay phone. There had to be *something* he could stand on. He looked around him.

All he saw was an old newspaper. That wouldn't work.

But maybe . . .

Georgie grasped a quarter tightly in his fingers and jumped as high as he could. Not high enough. He tried again. Not quite high enough. Again. Almost there! He jumped one last time, as high as he could, and tried desperately to push the quarter into the coin slot.

The quarter missed the slot and bounced off the phone into the bushes behind him, and Georgie knocked his elbow on the way down.

"Ow!" Georgie cried, grabbing his elbow. He'd hit his funny bone. *Ow ow ow ow ow.*

Georgie took a deep breath and tried to figure out what he should do next. Clearly he wasn't going to be able to jump to use the phone. Maybe he could pile up some rocks to stand on? He looked around him. There sure were a lot of rocks around here, but they were all *huge*. He'd have a tough time trying to move them.

Nonna Rosa was walking over to him, a curious look on her face. She was probably wondering about all the jumping and shouting.

Maybe he could get Nonna Rosa to help him move the rocks! That could work! She was big enough to lift them.

Wait a minute . . .

Georgie wanted to slap himself in the head. Nonna Rosa was *big*. Bigger than Georgie, anyhow. *She* could reach the phone!

Georgie waved her over to him, and then handed her the rest of the coins from his pocket and pointed to the phone. She seemed to understand. Nonna Rosa slipped the correct change into the slot. Good. Now came the tricky part.

"Dial this number," Georgie said to her.

"*Cosa?*"

But Georgie was ready. He held out his finger and jabbed at the sky, like he was dialing on a number pad. Nonna Rosa nodded that she understood.

"One," Georgie said. He held up one finger, and Nonna Rosa smiled at him and pressed the 1.

"Five," he told her, holding up five fingers. Nonna Rosa pushed the button.

They continued that way until Georgie's entire

phone number was dialed, and Nonna Rosa handed the receiver down to him. The phone rang and rang, and when his mother finally picked up and said hello, Georgie's heart leaped up into his throat and he felt like he might cry with relief.

"Mom!" he shouted.

"Oh, Georgie!" she cried. "Where *are* you?"

Georgie's mom finally found the store they were at in the phone book, and she came and got them. She drove Georgie and Jeanie home in her car, while Nonna Rosa followed behind.

"Don't you have any other clothes, dear?" Georgie's mom had asked Jeanie when she saw her.

Jeanie shook her head. Her cheeks were shiny with dried tears. "I accidentally left my stuff in my dad's car when he dropped me off at the pool," she said.

"Oh, honey," Georgie's mom answered, "you must be freezing!" Georgie hated that his mom was being so nice to Jeanie. He wondered if she'd still be that nice if she knew Jeanie had thrown a rock at him and signed him up to be Abraham Lincoln. "Why don't you sit up front?" she said. "We'll turn on the heater for you. Georgie, why didn't you let her use your towel?"

Georgie shrugged his shoulders and buckled himself into the backseat. But Jeanie had an answer ready. "He didn't give me his towel because he hates me," Jeanie told his mother. She wiped her nose with the back of her hand.

Georgie sat up straight in his seat, ready to defend himself, but his mom just chuckled. "Oh, I'm sure he doesn't hate you, dear," she said.

"Yes, he does," Jeanie replied. "I've been trying to be friends with him forever and a half, and he just hates me."

"What?" Georgie hollered. "You were *not* trying to be friends with me. You were throwing—"

"And when I try to talk to him, he calls me names. He calls me Jeanie the Meanie, even though I *hate* that."

Georgie's mom raised an eyebrow at him in the rearview mirror. "Is that true, Georgie?" she asked him.

"I don't remember," Georgie grumbled, slouching

in his seat to avoid his mom's gaze.

"He did," Jeanie said. "It wasn't very nice. Anyway"—she pointed at Georgie's mother's stomach—"I didn't even know you were going to have a baby. Georgie never told me that. When's it going to be born?"

Georgie rolled his window down so maybe the air rushing by would block out the sound of this idiotic conversation, but he could still hear his mom's response. "It's due in May," she said. "Georgie, can you please roll up your window? I have the heater on for Jeanie."

Georgie rolled up his window but left it open the smallest crack.

"I'm gonna be an obstetrician, you know," Jeanie said, holding her hands up to the heater vent.

"Really?" Georgie's mom said. "That's wonderful!"

"Or I might be an actress. Or a writer. I haven't decided yet."

"Well, you have plenty of time to make up your mind."

Georgie wished his mom would stop acting like

Jeanie the Meanie was a normal person, someone you could just have a regular conversation with in the car, someone like Andy.

Jeanie rubbed her hands together and then stuck them under her armpits. "I wonder what your baby's gonna look like," she said. "I mean, I wonder if it's gonna be short like—"

"Hey, Jeanie, I think that's your house!" Georgie shouted suddenly.

Jeanie looked out the window. "What? No, that's not it. We're miles away." She turned back to Georgie's mom. "Want to hear me sing an Italian opera?"

Georgie would have rather eaten live scorpions than listen to Jeanie's singing again, but at least they weren't talking about Baby Godzilla anymore.

After what seemed like hours, Jeanie finally pointed out the window. "That's it right there, Mrs. Bishop," she said. Georgie's mom pulled into the driveway, and Jeanie opened her door. "Thank you so much for the ride."

"No problem, Jeanie. It was a pleasure to meet you."

"G'bye! 'Bye, George Washington!" As the car

pulled away, Jeanie smiled with an innocent wrinkle of her nose and gave a friendly wave.

"Well," Georgie's mom said as she pulled out of the driveway, "she sure seemed like a nice young lady."

Georgie wasn't listening. He was tugging on the sleeves of his sweatshirt, watching Jeanie's house disappear around the corner. Up in the driver's seat, his mom's belly looked bigger than ever. Georgie stared at it, thinking. There was something he wanted to ask his mom, something he'd been wanting to ask for a long time. About Baby Godzilla, and violins, and . . . well, he wasn't sure what exactly. But before he was able to figure it out, they were home.

Late Sunday afternoon the doorbell rang. Georgie stayed in his room while his father went to see who it was.

"Georgie!" his dad called a minute later. "You have a visitor!"

A visitor? Who could that be? All at once Georgie had the sickening thought that it was Jeanie the Meanie, and he contemplated escaping out his window. But he slunk to the door.

His visitor was Andy.

"Um, hey, Georgie," Andy greeted him. He pushed his hair out of his eyes and shifted his bike helmet to his side.

"Hey." What was *Andy* doing here? Had he come to yell at him about getting his grandma lost in the middle of nowhere?

"Why don't you invite Andy inside, G?" Georgie's dad called from the front room. "You guys can play in your room for a while."

"Oh. Okay." Georgie led Andy through the hallway to his room, just like he had a million times before. But it wasn't the same this time. Because this time they weren't friends.

They sat down on the floor, Georgie leaning against his bed and Andy cross-legged, picking at the carpet. Neither of them spoke for a long time.

"I saw you got a new bike," Andy said at last.

Georgie nodded. "Yeah," he said. "Got it for Christmas."

"Oh, that's cool. Is it fast?"

"Yeah. It's a ten-speed." Georgie didn't mention that he hadn't actually ridden it yet. That he'd never ridden *any* bike before. That even though the snow was finally melting, Georgie just didn't feel the need to go outside on his specially designed low-seat bike and learn how to ride it. Who was he supposed to go riding with once he learned?

"Cool," Andy said with a shrug. He kept picking at the carpet.

I'm sorry about what I said, Georgie thought. He should just say that—even if it wasn't entirely true. Even if he was still a little angry. At least maybe then they'd be friends again. But he couldn't bring himself to do it.

"Hey, you want to stay over for dinner?" Georgie said suddenly. "We're having tuna casserole."

Andy looked up. "Sure."

"Okay," Georgie said. "Let me just check with my mom. Mom!" He raced into the living room. "Mom, can we please have tuna casserole? *Please?*"

She smiled. "Andy staying for dinner?" she asked. Georgie nodded. "I think tuna casserole sounds perfect."

"You can stay!" Georgie called as he ran back to his room.

"Cool," Andy said.

Georgie sat back down on the floor. Andy started

picking at the carpet again. Georgie stared at the wall. Andy rolled a piece of lint between his fingers. Georgie wondered if they'd ever be able to talk to each other again.

"Um," he said, "you want to go see if my mom needs some help?"

Andy shrugged. "Sure."

It was easier to talk to each other while they were chopping vegetables. Andy told Georgie and his mom about the weekend before, when he'd gone to the movies with his family and Nonna Rosa had fallen asleep with her hand in the popcorn bucket. Georgie talked about how he was starting swimming lessons and how his teacher thought he was really good. His mom just listened and nodded and smiled. She hardly said anything at all, but Georgie was glad she was there.

Talking didn't seem so hard at dinner, either, with Georgie's mom and dad both at the table. That was why, all of a sudden, Georgie felt like he could ask something.

"So, um, when are you moving?" he said. Andy didn't answer right away, so Georgie took a big bite of casserole and chewed nervously.

Georgie's father plucked another roll from the basket. "I didn't know your family was moving, Andy."

"Oh, um . . ." Andy took a gulp of water. "We're not. My parents were thinking about it, to move to a bigger house, but I think now they're just gonna build another room for my grandma."

"I see," Georgie's dad said. Then he started in on a long conversation with Georgie's mom about building codes and roofing, and Georgie had to stop listening before he died of boredom. He helped himself to another scoop of tuna casserole and glanced across the table. Andy gave him a small smile.

After dinner Georgie and Andy said they'd help with the dishes, but Georgie's dad insisted they must have better things to do. Finally Georgie suggested they play Lava Wars in the guest bedroom. They hadn't played in forever, and anyway, who knew how many chances they'd get before it became the baby's room?

After twenty minutes Georgie was down to only one arm, because the other one had been instantly burned off by lava when he'd accidentally touched the ground in an attempt to steady himself. He was doing much better than Andy, though, who had already lost a leg and was having to hop from the bed across the pillow bridge to the doorway. Then, halfway to the door, Andy slipped on a pillow and died in the sea of lava. Georgie was instantly declared the one-armed Lava Wars champion.

"Two out of three?" Andy asked.

"Sure."

"You know," Andy said as Georgie made his first attempt at crossing the pillow bridge, "I played this with Russ once. He stinks at it."

"Really?" Georgie asked. He tried to act like he didn't care at all. "How do you stink at Lava Wars?"

"He kept falling over. In, like, four seconds."

"*Really?*" Georgie tagged the doorknob and started on his way back to the bed.

"Yeah. He's not very good at making up songs, either, like you and me. We tried one time, but it was just boring."

It was funny, Georgie realized. Even though he'd thought of a million reasons why he missed Andy, he'd never once wondered what Andy might miss about *him*.

He made it successfully to the bed without losing any body parts, and Andy took his turn. "Russ is pretty cool, though," Andy said as he made the first leap. "I still think you might like him."

"Hey, Andy?" Georgie said. He knew he had to get it all out quickly, while Andy was looking the other way. "I'm sorry about before. About what I said and everything."

"Yeah," Andy said, still facing the door. He leaped to the second pillow. "I'm sorry too." And when he turned around, even though both boys pretended they hadn't said anything at all, suddenly it was easier to talk to each other.

An hour later Andy's mother called to say she was coming to pick him up because it was already dark outside. They waited for her on the porch, and Andy took a closer look at Georgie's new bike.

"This is really nice," he said. "It's way newer than mine." He examined the pedals. "You want to go riding with me and Russ sometime? We found this really great trail behind his house. We've only been once. You should come."

Georgie thought about it. "Um, okay. Sure."

"Cool. We'll go next weekend."

Andy's mother pulled up in the driveway, with Nonna Rosa in the passenger's seat. Nonna Rosa hopped out and gave Georgie a gigantic hug, babbling at him in Italian, and then she helped Andy load his bike into the back of the car. Andy's mother sat beside Georgie on the steps.

"Nonna Rosa wanted me to say that she is sorry," Mrs. Moretti said. "For getting you lost. And she wanted to say thank you too. She said you saved the day."

"Oh." Georgie shrugged. "Well, you know."

"You know what she told me?" Mrs. Moretti said. "She said you and she are not so different. You both have your trouble, but you learn to adjust."

Georgie nodded and smiled.

"And do you know what else?"

"What?"

"She is going to start taking English lessons. My mother. At sixty-five." Mrs. Moretti beamed. "She said if you could fight your battles, she could too."

"Oh. Um, that's cool."

She wrapped an arm around Georgie and squeezed him tightly. "I wanted to thank you too, Georgie. For helping my mother. You are a good boy."

"Uh, thanks."

Mrs. Moretti brushed herself off and helped Andy and Nonna Rosa with the bicycle. Then they all piled into the car and drove off, and Andy rolled down the window and shouted, "'Bye, Georgie! Don't forget about next weekend!"

Georgie raced inside and found his father watching TV. "Hey, Dad!" he said. "Remember how you said that when I wanted to learn how to ride my bike, you'd help me? Well, I gotta learn before next weekend. And I gotta be *good*."

All right, time for another favor. For this one you need a bunch of glasses and a spoon. They have to be real glass, not plastic.

Got everything? Good. Now fill three glasses up with water, one almost all the way full, one medium full, and one just a little. Then set them on a table.

Now, take your spoon and tap it against each one of the glasses. Just don't do it too hard and break them. That happened to me once.

Do you hear how each glass makes a different note? Pretty neat, right?

Okay, now empty out one of the glasses and refill it with exactly enough water to make a G note. Then fill up four more glasses with water for notes A through D, and play the "Ode to Joy." I'll wait here.

What? Having some trouble? Did you even <u>try</u>?

You probably think it's too hard. I bet you think it's impossible even, that no one can do it.

Well, Georgie can.

Just thought you should know.

The next week flew by. Even with play rehearsals for an hour after school and Jeanie the Meanie tap-tap-tapping on his shoulder every day, Georgie felt happier than he'd been in months.

In the afternoons at recess Georgie played kickball with Andy and Russ. Georgie was a pretty good kicker, even if he couldn't run very fast. At lunch all that week Russ was helping paint sets for the play in Mr. Myers's room, so Georgie ate with Andy and they made mashed-potato snowmen. Once Andy laughed so hard, he spit chocolate milk into his peas.

After school, when play rehearsals were over, Georgie's dad helped him ride his bike. He said he'd never seen anyone so determined, and Georgie learned fast. By the time Saturday rolled around, Georgie was almost positive he could keep up with Andy and Russ on the bike trail without falling over.

Georgie's mom drove Andy and Georgie over to Russ's house with their bikes in the back of her mini-van. Russ ran outside when he saw them coming, his bike helmet already in his hand.

"Hey!" he called, strapping on his helmet. "Let me help you with your bikes!" And in a matter of minutes they were off.

Georgie had to admit the trail behind Russ's house was pretty cool. It was on a hill, and it was dirt, but it was mostly smooth going, and there weren't too many rocks.

Actually, Russ wasn't so bad either. Even though Georgie wanted to keep hating him, he just couldn't. Russ didn't do anything horrible, and he wasn't *too* nice, the way some people were when they hung out with Georgie, trying to help him with every single little thing like he was a baby. Russ was just . . . friendly. So finally Georgie decided not to hate him anymore.

They were walking their bikes up to the highest

part of the hill when Russ said, "Hey, Georgie, did you decide yet if you want to help us walk dogs?"

"Huh?" Georgie said.

Andy was walking ahead of them, and he turned around, looking a little sheepish. "Um, yeah," he said. "I was supposed to ask you. Me and Russ need help."

"Yeah," Russ said. "*Loads* of help. I think maybe we advertised a little *too* much. Now we have too many dogs."

"Oh, yeah?" Georgie asked.

"*Way* too many," Andy replied.

"Well," Georgie said, thinking about it, "I guess I could help. I mean, I could use the money. But no way am I walking any poodles."

Russ grinned. "No poodles," he said. "It's a deal."

"Definitely," Andy said. "No poodles."

Back at Russ's house, after a quick lunch of grilled cheese sandwiches, they decided to make ice cream sundaes. They sat on the floor of Russ's bedroom and ate as fast as they could, to see who could get the worst ice cream headache, but they couldn't decide who won.

They were lying on the floor, empty bowls beside them and hands over their heads, when Andy sat up. "Hey, guys," he said, "I forgot to tell you something."

Georgie and Russ sat up too, but Russ was still holding his head. "What?" Georgie asked.

"Well, I practically *begged* my parents, and they decided that the new room they're gonna build can be mine, and my grandma will have my old room. Plus, they said I can do whatever I want to it, so you gotta help me think of something cool."

Russ chewed his lip. "You could have a teepee in it!" he said.

"Or maybe a hammock," Georgie chimed in. "That would be cool."

"Yeah!" Andy said. "Or what about a bed that's sunk into the floor?"

They spent the next half hour trying to come up with ideas for Andy's new room. Most of them were pretty stupid. Andy thought up giant people-size hamster tubes, and Georgie said he should have aquarium walls filled with giant squid, and still all Russ could come up with was a teepee. But when Georgie suggested a rock-climbing wall, Andy stopped to think for a moment.

"That's a really good idea," he said.

"Would it be a real one?" Russ asked. "With ropes and stuff?"

Georgie thought about it. "It could be. And maybe at the top there'd be a loft or something. Somewhere you have to climb to."

"Yeah!" Russ cried. "That'd be great!" He snatched a notebook and a pencil off his desk and began drawing, and Georgie and Andy crowded around to see. "Like this!" he said.

"Maybe there should be a regular ladder coming up the side too," Georgie suggested. "In case you didn't feel like using the rock wall."

Russ nodded and quickly sketched one in.

They planned the whole rest of the afternoon, and by the time Georgie's mom came to pick him up, Georgie realized he hadn't thought about Baby Godzilla, or Jeanie the Meanie, or Abraham Lincoln, once all day.

Two weeks later, Georgie found himself at his very last rehearsal for the school play. He watched as Russ gave his George Washington speech onstage. It was okay, but he didn't make it sound very interesting. When he was finished, Russ sat down in the audience next to Georgie, and they worked on their new dog walking flyers: "RGA Dog Walking. Absolutely the best ever (No poodles!)"

"Georgie!" Mr. Myers called. "You're next!"

Georgie shuffled up the steps to the stage and stood in the middle, right where Mr. Myers had told them to. He tried not to look into the audience, but he couldn't help it. Mr. Myers was there, and Russ of course, and all the other presidents, and a few parents and some little kids who were probably younger brothers and sisters, and . . .

Jeanie the Meanie.

What was she doing there? She wasn't in the play.

"You ready, Georgie?" Mr. Myers called. "I want you to give your speech exactly as you're going to say it tomorrow night."

Georgie had already decided that the way he was going to say his speech tomorrow night was as quickly as possible. He took a deep breath and tried to get all his lines out at once.

"Hello my name is Abraham Lincoln." He thought he heard a giggle, but he kept going, staring at his feet the whole time. "I was the sixteenth president of the United States and I was born in a log cabin in Kentucky." *Definitely* a laugh that time. It was probably Jeanie the Meanie. She had probably come just to make fun of him. "I was elected to the House of Representatives in—"

"Georgie!" Mr. Myers called from the audience. Georgie stopped talking and stood with his hands in his pockets. "I'm sorry, Georgie, but that's much too fast. We can't understand what you're saying. Try to look up a little more, too, okay? Why don't you start from the top?"

Georgie looked out into the audience and began his speech again, a little more slowly this time. "Hello, my name is Abraham Lincoln. I was the sixteenth—" He heard the giggle again. He turned his head quickly to look at Jeanie the Meanie, sitting all the way in the back, but he was surprised to see that she hadn't been laughing at all. Actually, she was frowning.

Georgie cleared his throat. "I was the sixteenth president of the United States, and I was born in a log cabin—" The giggles, Georgie realized, were coming from two second graders in the front row. Jeanie was still frowning.

"You're doing great, Georgie!" Mr. Myers called. "Keep going!"

Georgie was *not* doing great, but the sooner this mess was over with, the better. He finished his speech, finally, and sat down.

Mr. Wilkins picked Russ up as soon as rehearsal

was over, but Georgie's mom was a little late. Georgie decided he had one last chance to save himself from a humiliating death.

"Um, Mr. Myers?" he said, walking up to the front of the gym, where Mr. Myers was stacking chairs.

"Yes, Georgie?"

"Do you think that . . . um, do you think someone else could be Abraham Lincoln instead of me?"

Mr. Myers set down a chair. "Why would someone else need to do it?"

"Because I think tomorrow I might have the flu."

"Georgie . . ."

"I don't want to do it," he said quietly.

"Well, it's your part. You signed up for it, and you earned it, and now it's yours." Mr. Myers went back to stacking chairs, as though the conversation were over.

"But Mr. Myers—" Georgie began.

"I think you're just nervous, Georgie, and that's completely normal."

"But I never—"

Mr. Myers picked up a large stack of chairs and faced Georgie. "Would I have given you this part if I didn't think you could do it?"

Georgie frowned. "No, I guess not, but—"

"Well, there you have it."

Georgie went outside to wait for his mom. Maybe she'd make something horrible for dinner and he'd get food poisoning. It was his only hope.

He'd been waiting outside for about a second and a half when the door opened behind him.

"Hey! Georgie!"

Georgie didn't need to turn around. He already knew who it was.

"I said, hey! *Georgie!*"

"What do you want?" he grumbled.

Jeanie stood beside him and searched the parking lot. "When's your mom coming?" she asked.

"Soon," Georgie said. He looked at her sideways. "Why?"

Jeanie shrugged. "I'm gonna ask her to take us to the grocery store."

For almost a whole minute Georgie pretended he hadn't heard her. He was hoping that if he ignored her, Jeanie would go away. But she was still there, standing right next to him, scanning the parking lot for Georgie's mom.

Georgie rolled his eyes. "Why do you need to go to the grocery store?" he asked at last.

"*We* need to go," Jeanie corrected him. "I have an idea."

"For what?"

"For your part in the play. To make you not stink."

Georgie glared at her. "Jeanie, go home."

"I can't," she said. "I told my dad your mom would give me a ride home after we went to the grocery store. And she'll do it too. She likes me."

"Jeanie—"

"Plus you *seriously* need help. You are the worst Abe Lincoln ever."

"I do not need help!" Georgie hollered. "Especially not from you. It's your fault I have to do this in the first place, so I'm not going to let you follow me around and *help* me with it."

Jeanie sighed. "Look," she said, "I know you're mad at me for signing you up, but really, if you think about it, I did it for your own good. You gotta learn to get over your stage fright."

"Jeanie, I do *not* have stage fright!"

"Yes, you do. Otherwise you would have signed up for Lincoln in the first place. I could tell you really wanted to." She chewed on her thumbnail. "I shoulda just signed up for Herbert Hoover. I would've been really good."

Georgie stared at her. "I never wanted to be Abraham Lincoln," he said. "What made you think *that*?"

"Well . . ." Jeanie kicked at a tuft of grass that was growing out of a crack in the concrete. "You were just sitting there, you know, with that pencil . . . and I could tell you wanted to write stuff down, but you *didn't*. And I figured you wanted to be Abraham Lincoln, 'cause, well, who else would you want to be? You said he was the best president we ever had."

"What?" Georgie cried. "I never said that."

Jeanie nodded. "Yeah, you did. In our report, remember?"

Georgie actually laughed, even though he didn't think things were all that funny. But he had to admit Jeanie was right. He *had* said that.

"Anyway," Jeanie said, "I owe you one for saving my life that day with Andy's grandma, so now you have to let me help you."

"How did I save your *life*?"

She shrugged. "If it wasn't for you I would have been lost forever in the middle of nowhere, and then I would have frozen to death in my bathing suit and I'd just be bones right now."

Georgie rolled his eyes. "Whatever."

"See? I'm right. So you gotta let me help you with the play."

"Jeanie, I'm not gonna—"

"Nope," Jeanie said. She rolled her foot over the tuft of grass until every blade was uprooted. "I'm not leaving here until you say I can help you. Then we'll be even. Besides, *someone* has to help you or you'll look like an idiot up there. And it might as well be me who helps you, 'cause I've got performing in my blood."

Georgie sighed. What could it hurt? Jeanie couldn't

192

possibly make him look any worse than he already did.

"Fine," he said. "What do you want me to do?"

"Well," Jeanie began, "first we need to make you tall."

"*Jeanie . . .*"

"No, trust me. We can do it. I have a plan."

Georgie thought about it. Maybe Jeanie was on to something. And if, somehow, she could manage to make him tall, he should let her, shouldn't he?

"All right," Georgie said at last. "What are we getting at the grocery store?"

Jeanie waved as Georgie's mom pulled into the parking lot. "Coffee," she said.

"Coffee?" Georgie cried. "I thought that *stunted* your growth."

"Just you wait and see," Jeanie said. "You're gonna be taller than anyone!"

Even though Georgie hoped and prayed, he didn't get food poisoning. And Friday night he found himself backstage with the other U.S. presidents, as healthy as ever, trying not to throw up.

The thing that made him the most nervous—more than the gymful of people waiting to laugh at him, more than Andy sitting anxiously in the front row to cheer on his two best friends, more than Jeanie's crazy plan, even—was Allison Housman. Allison and the rest of her seventh-grade class were working stage crew for the play, and she was in charge of the curtain. Right now she was standing, with her pretty red hair framing her pretty oval face, just offstage, waiting for her cue to pull the curtain for the beginning of the show. She had the perfect spot to watch Georgie make a fool of himself.

And Georgie was certain that he was indeed going to make a fool of himself. The only thing he could do about it now was delay his humiliation for as long as possible. Which was why he was the only president not yet in his costume. Georgie figured he could get dressed while Ariel "Buchanan" Aubach gave her speech, so he still had a while to go yet.

At least Georgie wasn't the only one who was nervous. Russ seemed to be scared right out of his powdered wig. Georgie was trying to calm him down.

"I don't remember any of my lines!" Russ was saying. "I don't know my lines!"

"It's okay, Russ," Georgie said. "I'll help you practice. We still have time."

"Okay. Um . . ." Russ squeezed his eyes shut and said his lines at robot-slow speed. "Hello. My name is George Washington. I was born in 1932—"

"In 1732," Georgie corrected.

"Right. Um . . . I was born in Virginia. I worked as a survivor—"

"Surveyor."

"Right . . . and later I would attend the Constitutional Contraption—"

"Convention."

"Right." Russ stopped for a moment. "Hey, Georgie, how do you know all this stuff anyway? Didn't you do your report on Lincoln?"

"I just know stuff, okay? We're running out of time."

Before they knew it, Allison Housman raised the curtain, and Russ went onstage with a gulp. He actually did pretty well, Georgie thought. No big mistakes, and he hardly sounded like a robot at all. Georgie could hear Andy cheering for Russ in the front row when he was finished.

"You were great!" Georgie said when Russ joined him backstage.

Russ didn't answer. His face looked a little green.

"Russ? You okay?"

"I feel kinda sick," he replied, his hand on his

stomach. "Like I might barf."

"Like stage fright kind of barfing?" Georgie asked. "You can't have stage fright. You're all done!"

Russ was about to say something, but right then his face turned greener than ever and he hurried off toward the bathroom.

Georgie took a deep breath as Sylvie Norris announced that she was John Adams. Only fourteen more presidents to go, he thought, and then his life would be over.

He glanced at Allison to see if she was looking at him. She wasn't. She was talking to Cody Grummel, one of the other seventh graders who were working backstage. Actually, she wasn't just talking; she was *smiling* at him too. Cody was probably saying something stupid, something not even funny at all, and there Allison was, smiling at him. Now she was actually *laughing*! She tried to keep it quiet, so no one in the audience would hear, but even from his place in the lineup of U.S. presidents, Georgie could tell she was laughing. And now she was tucking her pretty red hair behind her ear . . .

Georgie couldn't take his eyes off Allison and Cody. The presidents went onstage, one by one—Thomas Jefferson, then James Madison, then James Monroe—and Georgie's doom loomed closer every second, but all he could think about was Allison Housman smiling at stupid, ugly Cody Grummel. Why couldn't she ever look that way at *him*?

They were all the way to James Polk, eleventh president, when Georgie felt the tap on his shoulder.

"You ready to get suited up, Mr. Lincoln?"

It was Jeanie the Meanie, and she was holding all the pieces to Georgie's bizarre costume.

Georgie pulled his gaze away from Allison and Cody. "Can't we wait until Buchanan?" he asked her.

"Not enough time," Jeanie replied. "We gotta hurry too. They're skipping Millard Fillmore."

"Oh." Georgie sighed. "All right."

"Here," Jeanie said. "Hold out your arms. I'll help you."

Georgie was just stretching out his arms when from behind him he heard, "Hey! Girl! Who are you?"

It was Cody, who had stormed over to them to talk to Jeanie. And Allison Housman was right behind him.

"I'm Jeanie," she said. "Who are you?"

"I'm stage crew, that's who," Cody answered. "Why are you back here? Are you a president?"

"No," Jeanie said, her hand on her hip. "I'm his costume designer." She pointed to Georgie. "I'm helping him out."

Cody snorted. "What? The midget can't put on his own clothes?"

Georgie bit his lower lip and looked at Allison, waiting for her to tell Cody to stop being a jerk, but she avoided his gaze.

"He's not a midget," Jeanie said. "Don't call him that. He's a *dwarf*."

"A dwarf, huh?" Cody laughed. Allison continued to look right over Georgie's head, pretending she didn't hear anything. Cody bent down low, so his head was even with Georgie's. "Well, if you're a dwarf," he said, "then where's Snow White?"

That's when Jeanie kicked him. Hard. In the shin.

Cody dropped like a bag of cement and shouted so loudly that onstage President Taylor stuttered and forgot half his lines.

As President Pierce, number fourteen, stepped onto the stage, Cody limped away, and Allison followed him. She never once looked at Georgie.

"Come on," Jeanie told him. "Hold out your arms."

Georgie did as he was told. By the time James Buchanan's speech began, Georgie's costume was in place. He set his top hat on his head and smiled down at Jeanie the Meanie.

"See?" she said, looking up at him. "I told you we'd make you tall!"

The audience applauded, and Ariel Aubach walked off the stage. Georgie's knees turned to creamed spinach.

"Go on!" Jeanie hollered. "It's your turn!"

"I can't do it," Georgie whispered down to her. He wasn't used to being tall. It was *weird*. "I don't want to be Abraham Lincoln. I never did."

"Oh, yeah?" Jeanie shouted. "So why'd I go to all this trouble anyway? Who'd you want to be so bad?"

Georgie could see Andy in the front row. He

couldn't go out there. He just couldn't. "I wanted to be George Washington!" he said.

Jeanie smacked him on the shoulder. It was as high as she could reach. "You goon!" she hollered at him. "You already *are* George Washington! Now go out there and be Abraham Lincoln!"

And so Georgie went. He stepped out onto the stage, one clomping footstep at a time.

CLOMP. CLOMP.

It was slow going, because of the three cans of coffee that Jeanie had superglued together and strapped to each of Georgie's feet. Plus she'd kept the coffee in the cans—"for stability," she'd said—so they were really very heavy, and it took Georgie quite a lot of effort to even lift them up.

CLOMP. CLOMP.

But boy, was he tall!

Jeanie hadn't stopped with the cans, though. She'd said that a dwarf just standing on top of some coffee cans would look *silly*, not like Abe Lincoln at all. The real Abe, she'd said, had worn pants at least as long as his legs. So she'd swiped a pair of her dad's nice black trousers, and Georgie was wearing those over the coffee cans, to make them look like real legs from the audience.

Jeanie had also said that Lincoln didn't have shrimpy little arms either. That's why Georgie was wearing her father's best suit jacket, too. And just so the arms of the jacket wouldn't flop around, she'd made Georgie hold on to two rulers, one in each hand, with white gloves taped to the ends. From the audience, Jeanie told him, they would look just like regular arms.

By the time Georgie clomped his way to the podium, he was sweating up a storm. But no one was laughing at him. At least, not yet.

He took a deep breath. *Here goes,* he thought.

"Hello," Georgie said. "My name is Abraham Lincoln."

No one laughed.

"I was the sixteenth president of the United States, and I was born in a log cabin in Kentucky."

Still no one laughed. Things were going pretty well! Maybe this acting stuff wasn't so bad after all. Standing three feet taller than usual, Georgie began to feel like a real president. He didn't even have stage fright.

"I was elected to the House of Representatives in 1846," Georgie continued, "and I later ran for senator from Illinois."

Maybe they weren't laughing, Georgie thought as he looked out into the audience, but they were all pretty bored. How could they be bored by *Lincoln*? Georgie wondered if he could wake them up a bit.

He raised a ruler and scratched at his black yarn beard. "But I lost," he said, and he put on his saddest face.

They did laugh that time, about half the audience. But it was *good* laughter. Georgie wanted them to laugh.

He clomped a few steps out from behind the podium. "Don't worry!" Georgie cried, and held up a glove. "In 1861 I became president of the United States of America!" He threw his gloved hands up in the air and smiled. The audience laughed again. A few of them even cheered.

"But then," he said, his hand back on his beard, "the Civil War broke out."

Georgie could tell the audience was actually paying attention to him. They cared what he had to say, and Georgie loved it. As he talked about the Emancipation Proclamation and the Gettysburg Address, even the youngest kids stopped fidgeting. When he told them about his assassination, many of them looked upset.

Everyone applauded loudly when Georgie was finished, and Andy cheered. Georgie tried to bow, but it was a little difficult with the coffee cans strapped to his feet. Instead he clomped offstage and waved a gloved hand, with a smart tip of his top hat just before he left for good.

After the play Georgie changed back into his regular clothes, but somehow he felt taller than normal, as though a little bit of coffee were still stuck to the bottoms of his shoes.

Georgie made his way into the auditorium to find his parents. Russ was standing by the door with his family. He seemed to be back to his normal color.

"You feeling all right?" Georgie asked him.

"Yeah," Russ said. He leaned in close to whisper in Georgie's ear. "Don't worry. I didn't barf."

Georgie laughed.

"You know," Russ told him, "I didn't even realize that was you up there at first. You were the only person who looked like a president at all!"

"Thanks," Georgie replied. And he meant it.

Georgie found his parents standing next to Andy in the front row, and he raced over to them.

"Way to go, G!" his father congratulated him.

"You were amazing," his mom said. She hugged him tightly against her fat belly. "I had no idea you were such a performer!"

"That was awesome, Georgie!" Andy cried. "Where did you get that costume?"

Georgie grinned. "From Jeanie the—from *Jeanie*," he corrected himself.

"Cool," Andy said.

Where *was* Jeanie, anyway? Georgie hadn't seen her since he'd gone onstage. He scanned the gym and finally found her at the food table, shoving cupcakes in her mouth. Georgie started to walk over to her.

But halfway there he noticed Allison. She was at the other end of the table all by herself. Cody was nowhere to be seen. Georgie could just walk up right now and talk to her. Maybe he could even make her laugh.

He took one step in Allison's direction and then thought better of it. Allison Housman might have been the prettiest girl Georgie knew, but Jeanie the Meanie was *way* nicer.

"Hey, George Lincoln," Jeanie said. "Good job up there." She smiled at him. And even though her face was covered in cupcake frosting and her ponytail was *still* just to the left of center, Georgie couldn't help but smile back.

"Thanks," he said.

"Oh, and I decided something," she said as she devoured another cupcake.

"What's that?" Georgie asked warily.

"I'm signing you and me up for fifth-grade drama. We're gonna be stars!"

On the way home Georgie sat in the back of the car as Tchaikovsky drifted softly out of the stereo. He looked at his parents, and he looked at the bump that was Baby Godzilla—15.7 inches and still growing—and he thought about the play. "I had no idea you were such a performer," his mom had said. And she'd seemed so proud of him.

Georgie knew what he wanted to ask about now.

He leaned forward in his seat and cleared his throat. He didn't want to say it. He *really* didn't. But he knew he had to.

"Um, Mom? Dad? Can I ask you guys something?"

"Of course, G," his dad said. "Shoot."

"Okay. Um . . ." He cleared his throat again. "Were you disappointed that I—" He broke off. "I mean . . . would you love me more if I played the violin?"

In the split second before his mom turned around to look at him, before his dad glanced at him in the rearview mirror, Georgie realized it had been a dumb question. Because he knew exactly how they were going to respond. "Of course not, Georgie," they were going to say, and they'd sound shocked he'd even asked. "We love you exactly the way you are. What would make you think a thing like that?" Georgie already felt like a moron.

But his parents didn't say anything right away. They didn't even open their mouths. Georgie's dad looked at him for a second in the rearview mirror, but snapped his eyes away quickly and lowered the volume on the CD player. And when Georgie's mom shifted in her seat, Georgie realized with horror that she was actually thinking about his question. What was there to *think* about? "Of course not, Georgie. We love you exactly the way you are."

"Mom?" he asked, his voice tiny. "Dad?"

They still didn't answer but glanced at each other, and Georgie's dad pulled the car over to the side of the road and turned it off. Then, slowly, he turned around to look at Georgie. His face was thoughtful, almost sad. He took a deep breath. Georgie took one too. "Your mother and I had always hoped you'd play some sort of instrument," he told him finally. Georgie's mom frowned and nodded slightly.

Georgie could feel his face fall. "Oh," he said softly.

He didn't look up again, but he could feel his father staring at him, trying to decide exactly what to say. For a very long time, no one spoke. Then Georgie heard the soft click of his mother's seat belt, and the next thing he knew, she had opened his door and squeezed into the backseat next to him, big belly and all. Georgie's father leaned back and put a hand on Georgie's knee. Georgie couldn't look at either of them.

"Playing music is something that makes us enormously happy," his mother said softly. "Both of us." Georgie shrugged, not sure he wanted to hear what came next. "It's . . . when I'm playing," she said, "when I'm playing music, I somehow feel . . . more alive."

Georgie pictured his parents in the living room, practicing their instruments, lost in their music the way they always were, and he knew exactly what his mom meant. He pulled his knee away from his dad's hand and scooted closer to the window, refusing to look up.

"So we hoped," she went on quietly, "we hoped you'd be able to experience that too. To be happy doing what we loved to do best."

Georgie continued to stare out the window.

"But Georgie? Georgie, look at me." He shook his head, still staring outside, but his mom waited, and finally he turned to look at her. She was smiling. "Georgie, you *are* happy. At least most of the time. You're a remarkable person, and who knows if playing the violin would have made you any happier? It certainly couldn't have made you any more remarkable. Maybe you'd be the world's best violin virtuoso and you'd *hate* it. So yes, that's what your father and I hoped for you before you were born. But now we hope bigger things: that you'll grow into the kind of person that *you* want to be." She wrapped him up in a hug, and Georgie let her.

"Your mom's absolutely right," Georgie's dad said. "But I think the real answer to your question, G . . ." He paused, and seemed to search for just the right words. ". . . is no. We couldn't possibly love you more than we do right now."

Georgie concentrated on smoothing out a wrinkle in his pants. "But do you think the—" he began. "Do you think the baby will play the violin?"

His dad raised his eyebrows. "I think we're just going to have to wait and see, don't you? You taught us that, Georgie, that you can't ever know what to expect. We'll just have to be surprised."

Georgie's mom gave him another hug. "That's true," she said. "Who would have thought our Georgie would turn out to be the best president in the whole school?"

At that, Georgie allowed himself a smile.

When they got home, Georgie went to his room, climbed up onto his bed, and looked over his walls.

Are you nimble with the cymbal?

Do you like to play trombone?

The thing was, Georgie realized, no matter how hard you worried about a baby, you could never be absolutely sure what to worry *about*. You couldn't tell anything from a bump in someone's belly or a couple of marks on a closet wall. Not really. The kid could be a musical genius, or a science whiz, or a champion skateboarder, and there was no way of knowing just yet. That was one thing the big fat book about babies hadn't mentioned: that no matter what you worried about, in the end you were going to be surprised.

For the rest of the school year it seemed like Georgie was busier than ever. He spent most of his afternoons walking dogs with Andy and Russ, or going to swimming lessons, or sometimes—not a lot, but sometimes—riding bikes with Jeanie, listening to her babble on and on about how great fifth-grade drama would be. To tell the truth, Georgie didn't really mind. He'd never admit it to Jeanie, but he was looking forward to fifth-grade drama almost as much as she was.

There was also Andy's new room to work on. It was coming together nicely. Between Georgie's great ideas and Russ's detailed drawings, the builders were able to figure out exactly how everything should go.

The first Friday in May, just two weeks before the baby was due, Georgie was sitting in Mr. Myers's class, feet up on his crate and back resting against his pillow, when he felt a tap on his shoulder.

Tap-tap-tap.

Georgie made sure Mr. Myers was looking the other way, and then he turned around. "Yeah?" he asked Jeanie quietly.

"You're being signaled," she whispered back.

Georgie turned. Sure enough, three rows up and two seats over, Andy was scratching his head with his pinkie finger. Georgie got up to use the pencil sharpener, and on his way back Andy slipped a note into his hand.

"What's it say?" Jeanie asked when he sat down.

Georgie showed it to her: "My mom's picking us up after school. The room's all done!"

"Cool," Jeanie whispered.

Just then Mr. Myers turned back from the board, and Georgie quickly pretended to be subtracting fractions.

Georgie thought he'd burst before he and Russ ever

got to see Andy's room, but finally they were there, standing just outside the closed door, with Andy's hand on the doorknob.

"Are you ready?" Andy asked.

"Yep," Georgie said.

"I mean, are you sure? 'Cause it's really cool, so you might want to prepare your—"

"Just open the door already!" Russ said with a laugh.

Andy turned the doorknob, and they all walked into his new room together.

Most of it looked like a normal kid's room, except with all new furniture, and new soccer posters, and a basketball hoop on the door. But the best thing by far was the rock-climbing wall. It took up the whole length of the wall—except for the ladder on the side— and there were fake rocks sticking out at all angles and ropes hanging down. The floor underneath was super padded, so you wouldn't break your leg if you fell off. That was Georgie's idea. The ceiling was extra high, and when you got to the top of the rock wall, there was a loft, just about the size of two beds. Russ and Andy climbed the wall using the ropes, and Georgie raced up the ladder. He got there first.

The three boys sat in the camping tent that Andy had set up in his loft, sleeping bags rolled up behind their backs.

"This is cool," Georgie said for the fourteenth time.

"Definitely," Russ agreed.

They stayed up in the loft for hours, reading comic books and talking about who would win in a fight, the Hulk or Spider-Man. They came down only once, so Georgie and Russ could call their parents and make sure they could spend the night. They climbed back up with a backpack full of food.

Georgie bit into a fresh-baked cookie and looked out over Andy's new room. And all at once he had a fabulous idea. He looked at Andy and then at Russ. "I'm gonna need you guys' help," he said.

One week later Georgie had a room of his own to unveil. He hadn't let his parents go inside his bedroom once since he'd started working on it, and they were more than a little curious to find out what he'd done. Finally Georgie turned the doorknob and let them inside.

"Oh!" his mom gasped, her hand on her enormous belly. "Georgie, this is fantastic!"

"It's great, G!" his dad exclaimed.

All Georgie had done, really, was repaint the room. That and write a new poem. Andy had helped him with it. Now, all along the top of the wall, in curves of words where the other rhymes used to be, was a new poem:

Were you born to be an artist?
Do you yearn to play the bass?
Do you want to be a swimmer?
Or study stars in outer space?

Are you dying to fly airplanes?
Do you long to be onstage?
Are you keen to be a gymnast?
Or write news for the front page?

Do you want to join the Yankees
And be known for catching flies?
Well, no matter what your talent,
We can't wait to be surprised!

All along the waves of the words, Russ had drawn tiny, perfect pictures: a paintbrush, some music notes, a baseball.

"Is this for—" Georgie's dad asked.

Georgie nodded. "The baby, yeah. I mean, if I can move to the guest room."

"I think the baby will love it," his mom said.

I'd like you to do me one last favor. Remember that piece of paper I told you to hide? I need you to get it.

Found it? Great. Now, take a good long look at what you wrote there.

The thing about me is

I want you to rip it in half. I'm serious. Rip it right in two. And when you're done with that, rip the halves in half. And then those halves. Keep ripping until you have dozens of tiny pieces of paper.

Did you do it? Good.

Now look at those pieces of paper and think about something. I don't know what you wrote down to begin with, maybe "The thing about me is I'm a good dancer," or "The thing about me is I have funny elbows." But I'd bet you a million dollars that for every tiny piece of paper sitting in front of you right now, there's at least one other <u>thing</u> you never even thought of.

Take me, for instance. I mean, besides being really great at singing operas, there are a lot of other things about me too, like that I'm either going to be an actress or a writer or an obstetrician. That's three things right there. Another is that I've read <u>Little in a Big World</u> five times. And I bet there are <u>tons</u> of things about you.

Anyway, I think you should keep all that in mind.

One week later Georgie saw his little sister for the first time. He smiled at her as she blinked up at him. She didn't look that scary at all. Only a bit wrinkly.

"What's her name?" Georgie asked his parents.

"Charlotte Marie Bishop," his mother told him proudly.

"But . . ." Georgie began. "I mean, that's pretty, but . . . doesn't she need a special middle name? So she can have someone great around her, to help her do great things herself?"

Georgie's father squeezed his shoulder and pulled him in close. "She already does," he said. "She has you."

Georgie knew that one day tiny wrinkled Charlotte Marie Bishop would be even taller than he was. And she might turn out to be a violin virtuoso, too.

But Georgie figured he could handle it. Because the thing was . . .

Well, there were a lot of things, now, weren't there?